INCOR ꓪꓳꓑꓔIBLE

THOMAS HUNTER FILES, VOLUME I

ANDREW MICHAEL
SCHWARZ

OTHER BOOKS BY
ANDREW MICHAEL SCHWARZ

Thomas Hunter Files
#2 Chapel Perilous
#3 Know Thyself

The Hidden

Prizm
Dominatrix of Sulan

Poppycock
A Midsummer Night's Mare
A Midsummer Night's Hunt

Novellas
The Demon of Montreal
Sharkbait and Other Stories

INCORRUPTIBLE

THOMAS HUNTER FILES, VOLUME I

ANDREW MICHAEL SCHWARZ

This is a work of fiction. All characters appearing in this work are fictitious. Any resembelance to real persons, living or dead is purely coincidental.

Vorpal Blade Publishing
PO Box 383
Renton, WA 98057

www.vorpalbladepublishing.com

Contact Andrew Michael Schwarz
at amichaelschwarz@gmail.com

Sign up for his newsletter at:
http://andrewmichaelschwarz.com/newsletter/

VORPAL BLADE PUBLISHING
vorpalbladepublishing.com

To Jennifer, who kept the original manuscript safe all these years.

If you don't get lost, there is a chance
you may never be found.

—Unknown Author

Chapter 1

Some believe we die gradually, day after day and year after year, each new birthday celebrating another year of dying. At first this appears quite morbid, but look at it a different way and suddenly, our mortal deaths make us eternal.

ㅋ ﹍ ﹂ꝏ

My client waited on the rambling porch of a prestigious Queen Anne revival.

"Mrs. Wengstrom?" I said.

"Mr. Hunter, thank you for coming so soon."

"Not a problem. Are you okay?"

"I'm fine. Thank you for asking." She looked a bit haggard, but I surmised this was more from situation than from age. Her body cut a fine figure under fashionable clothes, and her dyed hair did well to betray her years.

"So," I said, removing my beanie and noticing an absence of rain, "have you been inside at all today?"

"Well, just a bit before you came."

"You live here, yeah?" I indicated the impressive architecture.

"Sorry, I just got antsy when I called you and wanted to get this taken care of."

"Oh, sure. No worries." I spread my hands like a Catholic saint.

"Thank you. To answer your question: no, I don't live here. The house belonged to my father, who passed two months ago. Since then I've been having it cleaned and getting plans drawn up for the remodel." She must have seen the look on my face. She laughed. "Oh, restorations only! No way am I going to change one piece of this architecture."

"You grew up here?"

"Unfortunately, no. My father purchased it after the death of his second wife, but can we go inside?" she asked, owlish. "Lived in the city all my life but still can't seem to get warm."

"Of course. After you."

She eyed me suspiciously. "Aren't you going to get your equipment?"

"I'm sorry?"

"Your equipment. You do use equipment, don't you?"

"Right," I said. "Look, Mrs. Wengstrom—Diane. Can I call you Diane? I know what you've probably heard or watched, but I don't use any of that stuff."

"Oh. Well, isn't that how it's done, Mr. Hunter? I want to make sure we do this the right way, you understand."

"Look," I said, sucking in a breath, "if you want somebody to come in here and break out the Geiger counters and EMF meters and take pictures of floating dust and tell you they think they saw a shadow, be my guest. Who knows, you might even get on TV. Me, I don't use that stuff because I don't need it, and it doesn't work anyway. So, if you want a circus, you called the wrong guy."

I turned and started back down the steps.

"No!" she cried. "Mr. Hunter, no, I'm sorry! Come back!" She hurried to overtake me. "I didn't mean to insinuate…I'm sorry. Everyone said you were the best, and well, I will just have to trust you. Will you accept my apology?"

"I will," I replied, "if you'll promise to leave the exorcisms to me. My way."

She shot out a hand. "It's a deal."

I shook it and gave her a wary stare.

We walked back to the house, this time in a far more reserved manner. When we reached the porch she turned to me.

"I do hope you understand that this matter is quite urgent."

I stifled an unintended yawn. "They always are."

We entered to a wide stretch of cherry wood. I fell in love. Hardwood floors make my heart go all gooey. The woodwork didn't stop with the floor but spread all over the walls and furnishings. Dark, lustrous, oiled and loved by hand.

"What's to remodel?"

"It's the downstairs that's got all the trouble. Can I offer you anything to drink?"

"Sure."

"What would you like?"

"Anything."

"Just say the word. I have everything from—"

"Espresso."

"Oh yes, of course." She gave me a quaint smile, trying to lighten me up. She knew she'd gotten on my bad side and wanted to make amends.

I turned back to the woodwork, something that wasn't likely to set me off, studying the carved inlays in the crown moldings, the Victorian armoires with the fine china and silver, plenty on both counts.

"Your father knew his business."

"Here's your coffee." She handed me a miniature cup and saucer, which held two amorphous lumps of brown sugar. When she handed it to me, our fingers brushed. I wondered if it was intended. We sat down at the table, where I sipped espresso and tried to act like a hipster.

She laughed. "You always drink so dainty, Mr. Hunter?"

"Huh? Oh. Sorry."

"No! You're fine. I was just *teasing*."

Teasing?

My little pinky, however, had seemingly of its own accord, flipped out in the affected manner of some long ago guillotined aristocracy. Of course it hadn't just "done that." I could already hear the menacing little snicker.

Do that one more time and I'm going to starve the both of us for two days.

I wasn't thinking it to myself, I was telepathizing it to *him*, and by "him" I mean the body portion of me. The Animal. He's a body demon.

So, you wanna bang this old broad or what? Animal was saying inside my head.

That's just rude. My instant reply.

She's digging on us, man. If you end up crawling under the sheets with that and—

Shut up. "Sorry, I missed the last thing you said."

"I was asking you how long you've been ghost hunting."

I hate that term. It makes me sound like some jackass with an infrared camera. I don't *hunt* the dead; I don't eat them or mount their heads on my wall. I communicate with them and I hunt something else entirely more elusive.

"Oh yeah." I leaned back. "About five years, give or take ten months."

"That all? I would have thought longer, well, I mean from all of your notoriety."

"I didn't know I was notorious."

"Poor word choice. Sorry. You are very well known. I didn't have to look long before finding your number. I was told 'use Hunter' over and over again." She leaned forward. "And you really do have two different colored eyes, don't you?"

Okay, so fine, Animal was right.

"Look," I said, leaning in to meet her gaze. "Thanks for the coffee. It's damn good and I like it. Now, why don't you tell me what's been going on with regard to this ghost, so I can *hunt* it for you."

She nodded solemnly. "Of course, Mr. Hunter, my apologies."

"Start from the beginning, I want to know everything you know."

She detailed for me an entity with which she had had three or four not wholly unpleasant encounters. She described it as a floating "splotch of moonlight" with a girlish face that sometimes spoke.

"I'm sorry, it said the word *mine*?"

"Mm-aaa-hhh-i-nn-e," she enunciated. "I believe it meant the house."

"Gotcha."

"My God, I nearly screamed, but just like they say in books, I couldn't."

She was talking now with that high anxiety one associates with having "seen a ghost."

I raised a hand. "That's enough to—"

"I came right back the next day and picked up where I left off. I thought, if she comes again, I'll just ignore her, because Mr. Hunter, I'll be damned if I'm going to let a little ghost scare me out of this house."

"Did she come again?"

"Two weeks later. I spent the night again and was sleeping in the guest room and just like before, woke up. Only this time, it wasn't any splotch of moonlight, but that face just as clear as a living person."

"And?"

"Nothing. Disappeared. Just like that."

"Did it come back after?"

"Nuh uh."

"Ever?"

She shrugged noncommittally. "Not yet."

"Hmmpf," I said. "Sounds like a harmless imprint."

"I'm sorry?"

"A routine haunting—a spirit's residual energy that stays behind after death and haunts in a sort of repeat time loop."

"Oh!" she brightened up. "I had no idea there were categories."

"Oh yeah," I said. "Lot's a categories. Sounds pretty harmless. Anyway, I should probably get to work."

"Yes, it seemed very stuck."

"Yeah," I agreed, "stuck is a good word for it."

"Yes."

"Ooookay, so I'm gonna get working on it then."

She's playin' with you, boy. Takin' you for a ride. You about to be a kept man.

"Go to hell."

"Excuse me?"

I swallowed and pursed my lips, like an idiot.

She would never understand this relationship I had with my body's mind, that I was talking to an entity called Animal, who spoke in my own voice and often took over the motor controls of my mouth. I reached for a ruse.

"Why, I thought I saw the ghost!" I exclaimed with arched eyebrows. It was the best I could do on the spot.

"You what?" She sprung up ready for frantic action.

9

"I thought I saw the specter and tried to banish it. Oh, I'd better get to work!" I was overacting, but it was working.

She'd gone white as a sheet and sat back down all dismal and defeated in her mahogany breakfast chair.

I made tracks for the basement, where I guessed the Relic would be.

She didn't have to show me where the basement door was. I'd spotted it coming in. It was the only door that looked original. It opened to a rickety set of wooden steps, which fell straight down into gloom.

If the ghost didn't scare me, the steps surely did.

I got you, bud, said Animal.

My toes spread inside my boots, cat-like, and my thighs rippled in a strange peristalsis. I'd had no idea legs could do that. After, I was steady in the dark.

Not gonna thank me? he asked.

"Fuck you." I was still pissed, but aside from his asocial tendencies, Animal is the kind of guy you want on your side in a knife fight. The one guy you would take with you on a vertical cliff climb. A flex of muscle here, a quickened reflex there and voilà, he'd have you landing on your feet and running to the next death trap while making a snide comment.

The basement swirled with dust. I sneezed. Unfinished, yes, but not what I was looking for. I needed to find the oldest thing in the house, and I figured it would be down here. See, the upstairs was all new. New floor, new woodwork, carpet, paint, you name it. Remodeled. I wanted the original house. That's the part the specter holds on to. What I call the Relic.

That's my own term. You could call it the "Object" or, I guess, the "Thing."

"Relic" is more descriptive. Find the Relic, find the ghost. A cracker barrel slogan. It works a good ninety percent of the time. After that there are other ways.

I scanned the dismal dump. Lumps of dust covered stuff. Old mattresses, boxes, chests, sheeted furniture. The usual fare for such scenes. It bored me. God, it did. Hauntings had become so dull. It's always the same thing. You rarely get variety. It's equivalent to the private dick's matrimony case. You get tired of chasing cheating husbands.

I strolled through the usual terrain and let my dead eye take the lead. Dust, dust, sheet. Dust, dust, sheet. Dust, dust, blue fire tongues outlining a rectangular pattern.

Bingo.

"Third, is that all we got, sweetie?"

No change in the scene meant, "Yes." I stood back and did a quick eyeball measurement. Height and width of a door, yup, secret passage.

"Ani, need a kick," I said and then waited. "Hello?"

"Waitin' for Kairos, babe," Animal retorted, using my lips to say it out loud.

"Jesus Christ, you guys are slower than *shit* today!" I yelled.

Then it came. The kick. My leg jolted forward at a speed I would not be able to tell you, and struck the blue flames on the far right of the door, about where the doorknob should have been. I felt nothing. Plaster exploded and an old, rickety oak door opened in a yawning crcek, followed by a cold blast.

"Nice."

The feeling in my foot would return after restoration of cellular homeostasis, about fifteen minutes.

Couple things to know: I died once, a fatal car accident, and when I woke up I wasn't normal. I'd also forgotten everything that had ever happened to me, but for a single memory.

Afterwards, little by little, I'd learned that I had a bunch of weird fricking entities living in my head. I say "weird fricking" because that is the most apt description I have found to date. In time, I gave them all names. Or they had names and I discovered them.

Animal—or Ani—you've already met. Then we have Third, an entity that operates through my gray "dead eye." I address it by Third and actually the thing answers up to nothing else. I have to address it politely, because if I don't the little shit just tunes me out completely.

I'm not blind in that eye, but when I call on Third, she sort of hijacks the ocular nerves and changes channels. I get a spiritual overlay on the material world or really vivid visions depending on the application.

The best way to explain Third is like this: place a lens from someone else's prescription over your left eye. Then imagine it had a dark tint to it. Now note how well your uncovered eye sees. That's Third Vision, the eye that is not covered.

Kairos-Kronos: this is an entity that's two sides of the same thing. The Einstein of the whole operation, Kairos-Kronos is always performing some abstruse calculation as relates to space and time. You address him as Kairos if you want opportune timing and Kronos if you want regular timing.

There's one other, but we'll save it for later.

My nipples went hard. Sounds sexy, but really it was just cold in there. I walked through the doorway and found what I was looking for. The room had not been touched. It had been sealed off and entombed. Preserved.

"Interesting Relic," I said, "a whole hidden room."

The temperature was an indicator, too, but it could have been colder due to the vault-like placement downstairs. This is yet another reason why I don't use all those ridiculous gadgets. I mean, do I need an infrared thermometer to tell me my tits are hard?

"Bring that old broad down here, boy. Lay her out and…" Animal said, hijacking my lips.

"Bring Wild Turkey down here, uncap the bottle and—"

No response. Animal hates it when I get drunk, because it makes him go beddy-bye.

The room looked as though it had gone completely untouched since the former inhabitant had lived in it. I mean tintype portraits on the dresser, doilies and lace, Christian crosses (seven including the crucifixes), a four-poster bed with lion-headed posts and an old peacock toile chaise lounge.

"Well, well, well, quite a nice little haunted house," I mused, squinting to see the tintypes.

I stood back. On the wall hung a portrait of a young woman, who I knew to be our ghost. Pretty, but austere. No smile, wearing the black weeds of a widow and some horribly dull bonnet.

"Cheer up," I said and then proceeded to call her out.

I got nothing.

"Well, we'll pull up a chair and wait then." I sat down in a dust cloud on the lounge. If the ghost was around at all, in any form, this would surely piss her off and most probably flush her out. They hate when you use their stuff.

I yawned, then closed my live eye and said in a big, loud TV voice, "Nice little place you got here. I think I'll move in. Forever! Hah hah."

She manifested at the foot of the lounge, appearing from the gloom like a jellyfish floating to the surface of a dark sea. That same "splotch of moonlight." I didn't need Third to see it, per se, but through Third it was much clearer. Oh, I suppose you could call this phenomenon a globe if you were a ghost hunter. I call it the Medallion. Certain ghosts manifest certain things. Not very descriptive, but all in due course.

A Medallion is the interface between this world and the Other One.

It's a decorative and mobile stamp of personality, the final physical manifestation. The Medallion is made of energy and so it "survives" death, the more energy the more survival. This one was pretty solid.

It glowed, this Medallion, with the typical unearthly light. From one perspective, it looked like an old lady's profile in an oval frame. *Interesting design.* Then it occurred to me: a cameo.

Ghosts are funny. They persist in a sort of half-conscious state. Make them fully aware and they cease. I don't know where they go. The Great Other Side; The Big All You Can Eat Pancake Breakfast in the sky, maybe. Who can say?

The face inside kept shifting between young woman and old hag. Beautiful, then hideous and back again. It wasn't that she couldn't figure out who she was. It was that she couldn't figure out *when*. I didn't say anything. I simply trained Third on her.

Slowly and deliberately the mouth opened and with well-practiced solemnity and ham came a single long, drawn out: "*m-i-n-e.*"

I couldn't take this seriously.

"Okay." I sat up and, without taking Third off her, said, "Let's do this. Pu-lease."

Everything blurred and stretched out into a single, distant focal point. Then snapped back, and I was in.

The whole room was transformed. I mean, no more dust. Soft lamp light, yellow walls and, you know, life. Meaning the scene came to life. This is how you see a ghost, by the way—the real ghost, not the Medallion.

You have to "see" them through their "eyes." In other words, you have to be inside their mind, because that's where they live—inside their minds, their universes, their very own spacetime. I wouldn't know how to do it without Third.

I became possessed of a lot of residual data just being in that time and space. For instance, I knew Hoover was president. I knew times were tough and folks didn't really know how to deal with the economic crisis of the Great Depression. Just like that.

I could smell everything. The fresh lacquer, the breeze from— oh, there was a window in here too, wow. And I could smell perfume. I brought my gaze to the bed, and there she sat. Twenty-something years old and crying her eyes out.

I waited. She cried. She didn't see me. Sometimes they do, but not her. Too sad. I could smell her under her perfume, sour from stress.

Oh, crap, one of those. I already felt fatigued at the very idea of exorcising a suicide.

She sobbed for at least twenty minutes—that's real time and it seemed like five hours—and then I finally saw what she had in her hand, a little tintype. Gingerly as any mouse, I crept over and looked at it. A handsome gent there in sepia tones with a nice shock of hair parted all prim to one side. Then she started saying it, over and over again: *mine, mine, mine.*

Somewhere along the way here, I had gotten interested in this one. I think because I liked her.

I tried not to feel bad for her, but failed miserably. She stood up finally, after it seemed she'd cried out all her tears, and started taking off her clothes. She stripped naked. Not a bad looking woman. Small breasts with prominent nipples, a healthy plump to her buttocks, certainly not over-exercised in this day and age.

Though I probably shouldn't have been checking her out from

a voyeur's perspective, I couldn't really take measures to avert my gaze, since I was in the Third Eye trance. She was performing her past life, whether she consciously knew it or not, and I was her only audience in ninety years. The trick was to get her to go through the whole thing. Sometimes they just roll, sometimes you have to help them out.

She picked up a garment—ah, the wedding dress. She began putting it on. It took a while to do it all up because it was an old-school type with a huge, long train, a bonnet and veil and all the trappings. But she managed to get it on, and then as I had predicted, produced the slipknot.

Really I didn't want to watch this, but with the good comes the bad.

She dragged a chair out under—I looked up—a rafter. How convenient. This wasn't the original room, I knew that now. Basement wasn't built with the architecture. But I was sure it was all the original furniture, her photos and stuff. Probably her belongings had been shoved in here and walled up, forgotten. Diane upstairs had mentioned seeing her Medallion in the guest room. I conjectured that the new guest room may have been her old bedroom.

She looped the rope around the beam, climbed up on the chair and tied the thing around her slender neck. She whispered a short prayer between sobs and then stepped off.

Unable to remove my gaze, I winced. That sound, the poor thing choking, her legs flutter kicking in the open air. She knocked the chair so that it tumbled over sideways. She clawed at her throat. Her tongue bulged. I heard something pop. The last moment in those eyes told it all. She had made a terrible mistake.

I felt sick staring at her limp body, listening to the creek of the rope against the wood.

God, this was depressing. But we weren't done yet. The death, the heavy dark energy, hit me like a manhole cover. I got so tired and weak. The room went gray again and cold and, like a quick-speed nature decay animation, dust built up all over me. I exhaled steam and shivered. She was really getting into it. Cold equates to death force. Life force inverts when the entity begins surviving through its death. The colder the deader. No wonder that cameo—er

Medallion—had such staying power.

I kept Third trained on the ghost-corpse, which by now had decayed as if it had been in the ground. Not real life memory now. The imagery was slipping all over space and time, because the individual doesn't know what happens after death. Not like he or she does in life. Senses distort and time goes to shit, giving way to a lot of imaginary fill in.

The face was going from young woman to old hag to skull and repeat. They get fixated on the head and face for obvious reasons. This was the beginning of the Medallion.

I kept a steady gaze throughout the whole sequence: the before-death moment, the death and the after-death, but it wasn't lifting. I kept Third going for another fifteen minutes and still, nothing.

The sequence was stuck.

I had done several suicides and knew about how long they should take: forty-five real time minutes max. But the heavy energy surrounding us just wasn't letting up. It was hard to breathe too, like being submerged underwater with a crooked snorkel tube.

"Okay," I said. "How'd you die?"

No change, just the same repeat time loop.

"How'd you die?"

I wasn't getting anything.

"Third, can you do a close up, please."

Third vision zoomed in, extending out to the halfway point between my body and the ghost. I'd managed this awkward position before to good success. The specter cycled through another five times with no change. Usually, at this stage, once the death is done, you get the confusion and then the decay sequence and then the wrap up.

"Third, all the way. Oh sorry, *please*."

I got the universal sign for "NON": the circle with a line through it. Third's way of saying not advisable. If Third did this, I would not only be inside the ghost's space and time, but seeing through the ghost's eyes. It could be dangerous; you could get stuck just like the ghost and then you would become the ghost, i.e. it would kill you.

But that's a bit like saying, "If you play a dead guy in the movies you might believe it." I mean, how fast are you going to lose your mind?

"Go in, please."

Third obeyed and put me in all the way. Suddenly, the room shifted and I was looking at myself—my body—staring up at me. I had the distinct impression of being in two places at the same time.

God, do I always look so hostile in Third eye gaze?

From this ghostly view, my job was to see if there wasn't something that may be creating an anachronism and throwing the whole sequence off. Some important detail of time that was making this thing hang up. To be fair, I had done this before. The anachronism would be something I would just know, but I wasn't getting any new impressions from inside the ghost's "body."

"Third, I'm not getting anything," I said, watching my mouth move. I got the red circle again, flashing.

I was frustrated. It should work. If I left now, it meant I would have to come back, and by then the ghost would be twice as hard to get out. But more to the point, I had never encountered a case I couldn't solve. Not on a haunting. And to have this happen with this young woman…

A new visual popped up. Something completely unusual for a case like this. A shadow passed across one wall and up another. Not just any shadow, but something from another time.

The anachronism.

I watched the two dimensional outline of a huge, serrated appendage, like a monstrous shadow puppet, trail over one wall, angle at the corner and snake across the other wall. I got the distinct impression that it predated the Jurassic period by a couple dozen epochs at least.

That was the visual. It felt like a chain saw going through me. In truth, it was going through her, but it sliced and diced me both metaphysically and in reality. It was huge.

I screamed. Then blew a fuse.

<৲৹ঊㅋ

I woke up in Third vision with that red warning circle flashing obnoxiously over the whole room. I felt like I had woken up after sleeping through the alarm clock. The room, in its present-day state, lay empty around me. No ghost, no 1930s tableau and no crazy prehistoric tail silhouettes.

"Third? Animal?"

I needed a cup of coffee and a cigarette or five. When I moved to look at my watch, I gagged with a pain that stabbed me from neck to gut like an electric ice pick.

"Boss, Boss, you okay?"

"Animal, what in the hell is going on, can you assess this goddamned thing?"

"Yeah, one sec, Boss. Kairos, man, give us the jibber-jabber on what's up with Boss's accident!"

I slumped back and let Animal do his work. He interfaced with Kairos-Kronos and delivered up bastardized versions of original reports.

After some intense teeth gritting and serious nose grunting I managed to light a cigarette.

"Animal!"

"Oh, sorry, Boss. Kairos says we had an accident."

"What?"

"Car accident."

"Don't be stupid. We're not even driving. Third, can you shed some light on this, please?"

A second later Third delivered up an image of a mangled sedan.

"Have you guys all lost your fricking esoteric marbles? At least get me something for the pain. Ani, you hear me?"

"Kronos, gimme some of those things that make the hurt go numb."

It helped a bit, but it still felt like a knife was stabbing me in half a dozen places. And my collarbone throbbed.

I finally got a glimpse of my watch. It was almost two o'clock in the afternoon. I had been asleep on this dusty old chaise lounge for over four hours. Was I getting old or something?

I had to get out of there.

"Crew, let's go." I stood to a sizzle of agony. It shot through my lower back, neck and left shoulder. I gripped the side of the lounge and spit fury.

"Goddamn it, turn on the mother fucking endorphins!"

Kronos, the pain number-thingies, dude!

An anesthetic wave rippled through me, not enough to kill the pain, but enough to see straight. It must have been pretty bad to outlast two releases. Kairos-Kronos isn't known for being stingy on opiates.

Trying not to limp or grimace, I made for the door and saw *it*. A dirty, frilly ball. I kicked it and watched it unfurl.

"There it is." Threadbare and yellowed, the incriminating element lay like a rotting rag. "You see there? Find the Relic, find the ghost." It hadn't been the whole room after all, just the dress.

Mrs. Wengstrom rushed to the top of the stairs, owl-eyed and worried as any Jewish mother-in-law. I lumbered up the steps like a drunken zombie. She gawked at me and I realized that I must look a sight, covered in dust and cobwebs, the remnants of a girl's death.

But more than that.

"Get rid of the room down there as a precaution," I muttered. "I'm taking this. Otherwise you're good to go." I said it through clenched teeth and went straight for the door.

"Can I get you anything? Mr. Hunter, what do you I owe you? Mr. Hunter?"

I'd already left, limping over the lawn to my black 1997 Porsche Boxster.

"I'll send you my bill. Thirty day net." I tossed the grimy, old dress in the trunk and made a mental note to burn it. I flinched at the pain of opening the car door.

She was rushing up to me, holding the door open.

"Are you okay? You don't look so good. Should I call an ambulance?"

"Don't!" I pointed as if she were a naughty child and winced from the gesture. "I'm fine."

"Are you sure?"

"Lady—"

"Okay! You said something about a room?"

"Yeah."

"I'm sorry, where?"

I was so exhausted now. "There's a secret room down there. Say, you wanna—stop that! It's just rude. Sorry I was talking to the...thing. Just...do what I said, okay?"

Chapter 2

I could barely keep my eyes open. Luckily I was in the Box, a vehicle I could operate with about a thousandth of my brain potential. I pulled up to Starbucks and skulked in to get a fix, ordered a Venti and chugged it.

The caffeine shot straight to my heart, but the pain was still spiking through Kronos's opiate haze.

"Screw you guys."

I fired up a cigarette and pulled the glove box open. A glass vial of orange pills tumbled out into my hand. I took two.

I sat in my car waiting for the morphine to kick in, talking to "myself."

"What the hell happened back there?"

"Car crash," Animal said out loud.

"That's not possible Ani, come on. We were sitting on a couch. Third, sweetie, help me out."

An image of a crumpled coupe popped into view.

"You could at least use the same car."

For some reason this whole experience was lost on them, but I knew my crew. If they'd known anything else, they'd have told me.

"Fine, whatever, I'll figure it out some other way. But, Animal?"

"Yeah, Boss."

"That doesn't let *you* off the hook."

"You mean with that old broad?"

"Don't talk like that in front of people. Bad enough you project them to me."

"I was just playin'."

"It's not funny."

"Sorry, Boss."

"Yeah, it's 'sorry Boss' and all that, but you never change. I mean, you do that crap all the time."

"Feel bad, man."

"Do you? Do you really feel bad, Animal? Because I don't think you do."

"Don't wanna mess up our special brotherhood."

"Well, you might if you keep doing that. You know what? That's it. Kairos…Kronos, whoever, can you figure out a calculation to muzzle Animal when he's about to say something rude and embarrassing?"

"Oh, Boss, come on, man, you don't gotta get like that!"

I knew Kairos was working the calculation, but I couldn't see it, and he (if he's a he, I don't actually know that) doesn't talk.

"Third, show me what Kairos is doing… please." I got a mental flash of a line of calculations on a chalk board. One straight, long row of unrecognizable symbols. Then it stopped and another bizarre symbol appeared in Magic Marker on a white flashcard.

"What does it mean?"

Third flashed me a string of images. A dog muzzle followed by a leash followed by a dog biscuit and then finally a white guy in sunglasses calling out German command words.

"What she say?" asked Animal, who could never make heads or tails of Third's visions.

I shook my head and sighed. "Said I have to train you to be a good boy."

"Oh," he said. "How you gonna do that?"

"Wild Turkey."

⊐7⊐⅛

Three cigarettes and an empty coffee cup later, I got to Powell and Market. By then the morphine was working its miracle. I found parking and drifted into the Emporium mall where I could gaze upon shiny things and stare at women's asses.

I didn't know what had happened back there, but I also didn't know if I cared. I had exorcised the ghost in the end, and so I would probably just charge extra and call it a day. I was accustomed to the strange and unexplained. Shit, for the last five years that was all I had dealt with.

I walked around, looked at jewelry and jeans and beanies but didn't buy anything. Some days I go shopping and drop a couple grand. I love silver and hate gold and I have dozens of silver rings I never wear.

One time I bought a hookah and blew a G on flavored tobaccos. I sat in my loft smoking like the caterpillar from *Alice in Wonderland*, brewing pot after pot of Turkish coffee, reading Mary Shelley's *Frankenstein* and chatting on a Goth dating site.

I got another coffee and sat in a fake leather chair on the second floor, overlooking the foyer, watching and admiring. It was crude. I felt kind of greasy doing all this voyeurism, but it placated Animal. I didn't figure it was harming anyone, except me probably.

It was right about the time I figured I should hit the liquor store and go home when the complete ruination of my day took place.

She was cute. Probably early thirties. She had lank, brown hair and was wearing leather boots, brown tights and a red, cable-knit sweater that went down just enough. She had been staring at me from across the balcony, now she was walking up to me. She was one of *them.*

I had two options: run away or explain at great and painstaking lengths the condition of my faculties. I still hadn't decided which, when she stopped right in front of me.

"Tom? Oh my God, how are you?"

"I'm good all things considered," I replied, looking around for an escape hatch.

"Oh wow. You look…great. It's really good to see you. You doing okay?" She was nodding her head in a positive, perfunctory manner.

"Like I said, I'm good all things considered."

"God, you've lost so much weight."

"Yeah." Apparently, this guy who was me before, had packed on the gut.

"You're working out, too. I can tell."

I shrugged.

"And I guess you cut out all the—"

"Sugar, bread and pancakes?"

"Yes! I didn't want to say it, but yes."

"Yeah," I said. "I don't eat like that. I like meat and vegetables."

You see, Animal liked meat and vegetables and some comment he'd made when I first became aware of him, told me that he had done a fix up of the metabolism. Only he didn't call it "fixing the metabolism," he called it "souping up the carburetor." Anyway, I hated sweets now and when I worked out, I put on lean muscle mass really quickly.

She was studying me. Gawking at me, really. I sort of leveled my gaze at her and stared her down. Then it came.

"You don't remember me, do you?"

"Nope."

"You're serious? Oh my God, you're serious."

"I'm sorry," I said. "You're a nice girl. I mean you seem like a nice girl and you're cute enough, but I don't remember *me*, let alone you. What are you to me? My high school sweetheart?"

"Your girlfriend," she said, "well, before you and Stacey got together."

"Yeah," I said. "Stacey's dead." I wasn't mad at her. I was just mad at the situation.

"Oh God, I'm so sorry, Tom. I really am. I hate this. I—when I heard what happened—I mean—I feel terrible for you. Are you fine? Do you need anything?"

"Am I fine?" I felt that old, shaky thing come on. This really wasn't her fault, but once I get going, I fly off the handle.

Settle down, bud. Kronos, gimme a fuggin' hand on the boss's heart throttle!

"Am I fine? Oh, well, fine if you consider losing your mind is fine."

"I'm sorry, I didn't mean to—"

"Fine, if you consider losing your whole, freakin' life down the toilet is fine. I'm sorry, what's your name again?"

"Beth."

That look of horror they all get sooner or later crept over Beth's face, the don't-you-remember-me's realization of what they'd stepped into.

"I'm sorry," she said. "I didn't mean to open a can of worms."

"Yeah. Worms all over the place around here." Again, I wasn't upset at her, I was just upset.

"You see, Beth, it's a maddening thing to run into people all over town who can tell you more about your life than you could ever possibly hope to remember. So you kind of try living vicariously through the little tidbits of information you pick up in coffee shops and street corners. And after a while, it's those little tidbits that just drive you nuts, because you think, 'if only I could just remember what fucking happened!' My name's Thomas Hunter, I don't even know Tom."

"I'm sorry—maybe you're not the same person—"

Kronos, do somethin' with those little things that change the mood, dude!

"Yeah, that's an understatement," I said, petering out. Kronos had caught up with me and, with the morphine, cooled my engines pretty quick. "I'm sorry. Not your fault. I'm…not totally right upstairs and—I'm gonna go."

I stalked out of the Emporium and walked past a Bible screamer.

△⌐⊼☒↑

I cruised to Golden Gate Park and sat in the heated car for a while. Then I took off my watch and rubbed the scars normally hidden by the band. Sometimes they itched.

I didn't know where these markings on my wrist had come from. Drunken party dare? Maybe something more sinister. The one symbol I knew was a stem with two curved half-circles on top. That meant Aries and my birth certificate date confirmed that assumption. The other one, I had no idea. A triangle with a circle inside. Could be anything.

So there they sat—two ciphers, side by side, scarred into my wrist—about an inch higher than where a suicide would slash. At least I hadn't been one of those.

Golden Gate Park looked a dreary tableau as I walked around the wet grass and cedar chipped paths. I sat by the Japanese Tea Garden house and stared into fog. There was one memory I had that was older than five years. Only one and just a snippet, but it was the most important snippet of my existence.

I had to do this next bit. Maybe it was to me as cocaine is to the crack whore, but if I didn't get my fix, I was going to be in a whole lot worse state than mere drug withdrawal.

"Third—"

I paused. Did I really want this? I closed my live eye.

"Show me the memory. Please. You know the one."

It bloomed like fireworks. A brilliant burst of light and color. It soothed me instantly, warmed me from the head down and made my body thrum. I focused on the lustrous tangles of blonde hair and inhaled the scent. Such a sweet comfort, perfume and skin mixed, unable to be distinguished.

"Oh God."

This was a simple memory, but filtered through Third, even without morphine, it became a sensory cornucopia. I could call this up on my own, but with Third it was a three dimensional hologram I could all but live in. No memory compared to the enlightened vision-magick of my Third eye consciousness.

I felt the pallor restore to my cheeks, the strength to my hands and a single tear slide from the corner of my eye.

"Oh, babe."

This memory was the one link I had to my past. Somehow I knew her, and if I could just find her, I could find everything else, too.

Then the memory started moving, and in it she was talking, but I couldn't make out the words. I never could. I couldn't see her face, either. Oh, I'd tried to dredge up the image of her face before. No luck. Just her hair, skin and body. I could hear the laughing, though, and I could feel the happiness.

And that's what I needed.

The light wreathed her in an enchanting glow, an angel in the sun. She lay on white linens. A dream finger traced her neck line, while my actual finger traced the air—down, down to her shoulder, then across to the intricate, naked faerie tattoo with those delicately inked wings all spread out to catch the imaginary wind.

"I need you so much." I was on my knees. Hadn't realized I'd gone to the ground, but I was crouched, biting a knuckle, tears streaming.

You okay, Boss? Can't see what's the matter.

"Not now, Animal."

The vision began to fade.

"Don't you fade it on me, Third. Please don't!"

It vanished And was replaced with an image of a red first aid cross. Who was she? I hadn't a clue.

"Ani, take me back to the car."

Animal walked us back. It's kind of like riding piggy back. You feel the motion, but not the legs.

Safely seated in the Box, I took the body back and turned the key—I would never let Animal drive. I crawled home through the tapering rush-hour traffic. The sunset came, short and pink, and I scarcely noticed it. Nevertheless, San Francisco twilight restored me. I could forget a lot of things at this time—as if I needed to forget more. I put my attention on the city. Then I pulled up to the warehouse.

My accident had brought with it a few possessions. One of them was an old brick warehouse at the end of Bluxome Street, in the SoMa District. When I'd moved in, I'd renovated the shit out of it.

I keyed in the entry code and pushed past the double-paned, wrought iron doors. I didn't bother flipping on the lights in the foyer. I knew every inch of the bare drywall and stripped wooden stairs in this still unfinished portion of the house.

I walked through the icky part and entered my sanctuary, an enormous flat with rough, brick walls, exposed beams, iron support girdles and a beautiful ironwood floor. I love thick, white bearskin rugs, so I use three giant ones to soften the tone.

Next is the big deal about the whole place. I flicked the light switch and let the muted LED lamps transport me. These lights were the real stroke of genius. Built-in wall fixtures cast a deep, cobalt blue band all around the circumference of the ceiling, like some North Pole aurora borealis. And above it, in a splatter of irregular and uncountable motes of light, engineered to fool the senses and deliver the soul, hangs a perfect night sky.

I was home. Already I felt the edge coming off as I stood under the living room sky and let my mind go. I would probably have stood there all night if not for my fingers, which snapped together in the pen-holding posture.

"Give me a minute, will ya?"

I'd knocked big, oval holes into the brick wall that had divided the two bays and trimmed all around the apertures to make Old World Gothic archways. In the bathroom, I'd spent a ton on granite, under-tile floor heaters, a jet pool tub, a dual showerhead, lion shower fixtures, you name it. Well, you could take a crap in splendor, I guess.

Basically, every room was huge beyond my needs and lavish beyond reason except for, oddly enough, the loft—aka my bedroom.

An iron staircase spiraled up to the narrow space. I went upstairs and kicked off my boots, sat down at the antique bureau. I set my bottle down with a loud tap. My fingers were going spastic and my hand was jerking in neat revolutions.

"Hold on!" I pulled out a leather-bound volume, turned to where the ribbon had kept the place, picked up the self-inking quill pen and off we went:

> Obnoxious Entity: *You shouldn't have been so rude in the mall with Beth.*
> Me: I'm sorry, I flew off the handle.
> OE: *You made a fool of yourself. People were staring at you. Not to mention, it's bad for business.*
> Me: I've got plenty of money.
> OE: *You keep spending like you have and you'll dry up the trust.*
> Me: I already have an accountant.
> OE: *And you really need to stop using Third for self gratification.*
> Me: You make it sound so sleaz—

We were interrupted by the sudden leap of a purring and very black visitor.

"Charcoal, you mother lover, you scared the bejesus out of me." Then, to the person behind me who had let the cat in, I said in a much more subdued tone, "You're here."

"That's all I get for being the first flesh and blood you've spoken to today?" The scent of Eva's sandalwood pervaded the room. I groped Charcoal's nape like a bath sponge and sent the little

Russian Black into a somnolent daze. He licked at my hand and then pretended to bite my knuckle. We both knew he could rip my throat out anytime he wanted.

I looked up as Eva plopped down on my bed. She was wearing a dress of vintage, black lace. She'd colored her hair raven, over her already natural dark, so it was really black. And she had on deep blue eye shadow. She liked to play up rich, dramatic colors against her pale skin, a kind of art. The dress left an open V across her chest where her cleavage peeked out voluptuously. The arms laced down all the way to her wrists. Typical for Eva.

"I thought I smelled you when I came home. You've been in and out."

"That doesn't sound very flattering," she said, leaning back on her arms.

"Sorry."

"Well, you look like shit."

"*That's* flattering."

"Touché."

"I meant your perfume…or soap. You witches wear a lot of that sandalwood, don't you?"

She sighed. "Ten minutes in a Wiccan store and suddenly you're a witch trial magistrate?"

Charcoal was lost in some feline heaven now, purring and sinking his claws through my jeans.

"Doesn't that hurt?"

"Feels sexy," I lied.

"So, did you have some shitty day or what?"

"I look that bad?"

"Thomas, you're wearing a scowl that I could feel from outside," she said.

"Oh, that reminds me. How did you get in?" I said.

Another sigh, but with a smile. "Magick."

"Charcoal got inside and opened the door." She had a key, but we both pretended she didn't.

"What happened?" she asked.

Now I sighed and finally sat back and let the cat sleep on my lap.

"Well," I said, "it started out fine. Had a house call and everything was going along according to plan. Then the lady said something that pissed me off, but I brushed it aside." I paused.

"Uh huh?"

"Then I did my thing."

"Divined the ghost and got it to leave."

"Yeah, 'cept we don't call it divining. We call it looking for and finding."

She shrugged.

I proceeded to tell her the whole rest of the tale, leaving nothing out except how I went and got all twisted on a Third Eye memory and cried in my car for ten minutes and then bought two pints of whiskey.

"It felt like it was trying to cut me in half or cut something out of me. Luckily Kairos blew a fuse and I disconnected."

"Ugh, that worries me," she said. "You take too many chances out there."

"Yeah," I agreed, lamely.

"What do you think it was?"

"I don't know. Some kind of—"

"Demon?"

I shook my head. "I didn't want to say it, but…maybe."

Demons—real ones, not entities like Animal and the crew—weren't something I knew much about.

I'd done a fair amount of cop work on weird murders, and I'd done a ton of house exorcisms, but demons were mainly the province of the Church. I just didn't deal with them that often.

"Are you going to report it?"

I shrugged. Then winced. "Probably not."

"Should you?"

"I don't know."

"Maybe you should go to the doctor."

"Fuck doctors."

"Thomas!"

"I'll be fine. God, between you and Animal, it's a wonder I can get a hangnail."

"What does he say about this injury?"

"Who, Animal? Nothing. Well, actually he says it's from a car crash."

"From today?"

I squeezed my forehead. "Has no clue."

Then she pointed at my bottle and said, "So that stuff really put's 'em to sleep?"

"Yeah, except the one. I have to drink like two bottles of the shit to make the obnoxious one go beddy-bye."

"You mean Conscience?"

"Yeah," I said and pointed awkwardly—I was just beginning to feel the drink. "All went to bed except little Conchy poo."

"And what does...*she*...say?" Then her eyes went wide. "Whoa!"

"What? Oh shit!"

My hand jerked madly, and I about fell off my chair. At some point in our conversation, I had rested my arm on the table, with my writing hand on the open diary. Now that hand was suddenly animated, scribbling madly.

Eva sprang up and rushed over. Her pale and very pleasing cleavage took stage directly at eye-level, and I had the dickens of a time yanking my gaze away.

We both watched as my hand wrote left to right in quick jerks and hooks, somehow producing a wonderfully smooth and legible copperplate.

"I'm always amazed at this," I said.

"God, Thomas that's..."

> *Thomas Hunter needs help. He is literally falling apart and won't admit it. This man is not a) happy b) in control of his life, or c) handling his vices very well. He is self-medicating with a variety of substances including alcohol, nicotine, morph—*

I pulled my hand away, making it scrawl an empty cursive into the air.

"Conch!" I shouted, while simultaneously losing control of the cat, who leapt from my lap—no doubt drawing blood—at which point I burst into hysterical fits of glee, watching my hand flop around like an airborne mackerel.

Finally I yelled, "Conch, come on, you sound like my fricken' grandmother, stop it!" The hand dropped to my lap, twitched and returned to my command.

Eva's eyes had grown round and she was shaking her head all forlorn, which made me practically pee my pants with laughter. Slowly, with the elegance of a cat, she sat back down on the bed and eyed me with wary suspicion. Charcoal was up and orbiting her, tail cocked, leaning into her and falling all over himself.

"What's happening to you, Thomas? Now, I really am worried about you."

"I need to finish this bottle. That's what's happening."

"It's not funny." She stroked the cat vigorously, if not violently. "You need help. I could see it when I came in here, and *this* just proves it."

"I'm fine."

She was shaking her head. "No, you're not. Oh God, you need help. Maybe you should see a doctor."

I laughed. "I would make that kind of doctor go cross-eyed." She was shaking her head and staring at the floor.

"Oh Eva, please!" I groaned.

"I don't know. Maybe you should see someone about all those..." she trailed off.

"What? Voices in my head?"

She shrugged.

"Look. If I thought my crew was really the cause of my, shall we say, unhappiness, I would go down to the cathedral and get them exorcised right now. But it's not my stupid crew. I used to think it was, but then I learned how to talk to them. You think I'm bad now, you should have seen me in the beginning.

"They're like family now. They don't harm me. They help me. For all I know, they're really just portions of my mind that spun off and became their own sentient voices. If you were to ask for a scientific explanation, I would say that one."

"I'm not asking for a scientific explanation," she said.

"You're not, but a doctor would. He'd note it all down in his little book and say, 'Mr. Hunter, can you tell me more about how you wanted to make love to your mother when you were two?' And I would say, 'Gee Doc, I would, but I can't quite remember her.' And he'd say, 'Oh, well maybe we should be looking into your amnesia instead of your fucking paranoid schizophrenia.'"

"Stop it."

"Well? Am I right or what?"

"Sure."

"All I'm saying is that if I thought my crew was the problem, I'd dump 'em. But I think my real problem is my memory. My *lost* memory…ah, whatever.

"What?"

"Nothing."

"What?"

"It's just…I do sound crazy."

"No, Thomas, that's not my point."

"Who else do you know whose hand does this? And who—who talks to his *body?* Who can't remember *anything* about his past?"

The silence that ensued became unbearable. I didn't want to say it. I was trying not to think it. Eva broke first.

"It's all about *her* isn't it?"

"Do not go there." The whiskey was hitting me now. I was well on my way down the drunk chute.

Eva was sitting there shaking her head and staring off into space. I knew we had just crossed the line. Then she said, "I hate you."

I took another swill of booze.

"God" —she was talking to no one now— "I love you so much I hate you. I don't know how that's possible, but it's true."

I covered my eye with the heel my hand in that all familiar expression of emotional agony.

"Oh please, Ev, don't do this. Not now. Please, please don't put me—yourself—through this again."

"You're just so fucking clueless, aren't you? No, that's the wrong word. You're so fucking lost. Jesus, Thomas, I see it now. You're so lost."

I couldn't bring myself to say anything. It was true. That is how I felt all of the time. There was nothing new going to come from this conversation. We'd done this before. A lot. It always went this route, and there was never a destination. I didn't have the energy tonight.

"Please, Eva. Please, please, please can we just talk about this in the morning? I'm sorry, okay? I would fix it if I knew how. You're right, I need to do something. I know that. I will, but not now, not tonight."

"I just hate seeing you destroy yourself," she said. "I don't know, maybe if you didn't have all those voices in your head, maybe you'd be better off."

I shook my head wearily. "Not the problem. They're not the problem. If they were, I'd be the first to chase 'em out. I just want my life back. I want my memory back."

"You want *her* back," she corrected.

I was swallowing tears, staring down into nowhere.

"I'm sorry," I whispered.

I felt her thinking. After a long moment she said, "Me too." I couldn't look at her. I wanted to bawl. I felt the air stir with her sweet sandalwood. She leaned over me and kissed my forehead, while slipping the near empty bottle from my fingers.

"Get some sleep," she whispered. "I'll call you tomorrow. Come on Coal."

Then she was gone. And once again, I was alone.

Chapter 3

Eva and I had a history. It wasn't a very long one, but it'd had its highs and lows.

I met her online. She was a Goth girl I'd chatted with when I'd done my hookah binge.

She was the only one who looked, for lack of a better word, normal. Kind of stupid to say of a Goth dating site. I went on there because I figured I'd have a better chance with a chick that was into occult books or witchcraft or singers that looked like mechanical toys, because they might have a better understanding of a guy like me.

I browsed the hell out of that site and "poked" a bunch of girls—actually still don't know what that means—and chatted and flirted, but I just wasn't that Gothic. You can take a good idea too far.

I must have been on day two of Death by Hookah when I found her. She looked cute in her little thumbnail photo and said she was Wiccan, which I liked. She didn't say "witch" or "succubus," just "Wiccan with about half the eye liner."

Her photo sat between Drkgerl666 and Gthkqn69: Eva88, for infinity times two (she told me later). So I sent her a message, which she answered, and then we got to chatting. I told her who I was and what I did and how I'd lost my memory, and everything I'd promised myself I wouldn't tell some random Goth girl online. She was fascinated. She had so many questions. Before I knew it, it was three in the morning. When I had to sign off she told me "sweet dreams." I never forgot that. Of all the things women have ever said to me, I've never forgotten that.

I woke up the next day and had messages from her. I signed back on and the chat started all over again. She told me about growing up and "oh, I'm twenty-six by the way, how old are you?"

Her mother had disowned her. She'd gotten emancipated on her fifteenth birthday. She made soap. We chatted and chatted and fell in love. I drank so much coffee just so I could stay awake and keep typing. We sent photos back and forth. She looked cute in her frilly, vintage dresses and her jet colored hair. She carried a little extra love but it looked to be in all the right places, and every picture she sent showed the tops of her white bosoms. The more I looked at them, the more I wanted them. At the end of the second night—somewhere around four in the morning—I told her I had to go to bed, and she asked if she could come over.

She arrived in an old, beaten up sedan and stepped out carrying a big, black cat in her arms. She laughed and ran to me and said she hoped I wasn't allergic to cat hair. She looked radiant in a metallic, purple dress; radiant in the predawn dark.

I took her up to the main room, turned on the starry sky, put canned tuna in a bowl and together all three of us lay on the white, bear skin rugs and stared into all those lights. She kept saying how she could see the constellations in them, which I didn't believe.

Finally, as the sun was coming up and casting its pale light upon the city, she rolled over onto my chest and kissed me. We opened our mouths to one another. It was an easy thing to pull down the narrow top of her dress and kiss those plump breasts.

Days passed in this way. We shared the hookah, drank whiskey straight from the bottle and ate pizza. I made a litter box from a sandbag and cleaned out my store of canned tuna.

My crew didn't make voices in my head. No blinding visions from Third. No juvenile comments from Animal. No wayward ghosts looking for deliverance. Just me and this girl—me and this pretty, twenty-six year old girl and her wonderful cat, who purred and meowed and rubbed against us when we slept.

I was never sure why the crew had stayed so quiet, slept so easily in those short days. But somehow I'd known they were there, and I'd known they were as happy as I was.

Three days flew by before I realized how fast we were moving.

What about the only memory of the one person I wanted more than anything? Who I missed more than life itself? What was I doing? Then it just seemed like I was in over my head.

Then the phone rang and I had a case. She had to go back to

work, and Charcoal needed his cat food and his mice to hunt. So I put the hookah on a shelf, and Eva kept a key.

ᄀᄆᆞᅡᄀ

"Hey, Doug. Thomas Hunter."

The sun was shining through into the warehouse main room and warming the ironwood floor. I had powered up my smart phone and called Doug Walser. I should say "Captain Doug Walser," of the San Francisco Police Department, Paranormal Investigations.

"Hunter! How are you, man? Christ, it's been a while!"

"Yeah, I know."

"You ready to get back in the game, bud? Aren't getting bored out there, are ya?"

I pulled at my hair nervously as I paced the floor. I'd just woken up and decided to give Doug a call. I had nothing prepared.

"Well, I was wondering if you had anything for me. You know, something juicy."

"Something juicy, eh?"

"Yeah, you know, something to sink my teeth into."

"You feel ready to come back?"

"Yeah, I feel pretty good. I'm just—the haunted houses are driving me batshit …bored." I was very careful not to say "crazy."

"Anyway, if you could keep your feelers out, I'd be, you know, interested."

"I hear ya," he said, slowly. "Hunter, lemme call you back. Just keep your phone on, will ya?"

"Sure thing."

He hung up. This was good, I thought. Could be good. Maybe. Way better than a flat "no," right? He had something. Now, he was checking it out to see if they'd want to bring me in on the case. Me, specifically.

I thought about calling him back and expounding on how incredibly well I was doing, but I figured that would look too eager and prove me a liar. I had to wait.

I lit a smoke and thought about the possibility of getting on a case. I wanted that. I really wanted to just drown myself into work—work I was interested in. To hell with everything else, just get my head into something and forget about all the craziness for a while. The phone buzzed. I rushed to the couch where I'd tossed it.

It was Eva. I answered.

"Hey."

"Oh my God. You answered."

"Yeah."

"How are you feeling?"

"Better." I looked at my watch; it was three o'clock. "Slept for a long time."

"But you feel better?"

"Yeah, the pain is a lot less today."

"You know who this is, right?"

"Yeah, the timeshare people," I said.

"Well, do you want a timeshare or what?"

"No."

"Well, I wouldn't sell you one anyway."

"Okay."

"Thomas, stop it!" she giggled. "I just wanted to say I was sorry for last night."

"It's all right. You didn't do anything wrong."

"Are you going to be leaving your hovel anytime soon?"

"Maybe. I don't know. Why, you wanna do something?"

"Only if you do," she said.

"I'm waiting for a call from Walser. I'll probably go out and get coffee later. If you're around, I'll pick you up."

"Okay. Walser, huh?"

"Yeah," I said. "I need a change of scenery."

We bantered a bit more and then said our adieus.

If he hadn't called back by now, he wasn't going to until tonight or tomorrow. I knew he was getting approval. He'd call me back whether he got it or not. The wait was the agony.

I hated the fact that he had to "get approval." It made me feel like a juvenile delinquent. I was probably the best paranormal investigator they'd ever had. I don't say the best investigator, just the best PI.

My lead had cracked the last case I'd done, but things had gone sour after I blew up at one of the directors and threw a pen cap at a photo of his daughter. Of course, that had been after a long string of expletives about the director's wife and mother. It was bad, but he had pissed me off something awful. And I was drunk at the time. So, I got what they called "time out," after which I decided I didn't need any of them anyway. And so, now I needed approval.

They weren't going to give it to me. Suddenly I became dead certain of that.

I ate some cold chicken and made another cup of coffee. By the time I showered and made it over to Eva's place, it was about five thirty. She got in the car on a cloud of jasmine perfume and held Charcoal on her lap. Somehow that cat didn't mind riding in the car. I felt glad to see her. Her smile made me want to smile.

"What?" she said.

"You look really pretty," I said.

She batted her eyes playfully. "Why thank you, Detective Hunter."

I shifted out of neutral and peeled away.

"Where you wanna go?"

She shrugged, so I took Brannan to the Embarcadero and went up to Pier 39, Fisherman's Wharf. The sun had come out, which made the wharf appealing.

Eva had been making soap all day. Her soaps were her third best seller behind coffee beans and magick books. They also had the added benefit of being inexpensive. She made all kinds: money soap, love soap, happy soap, help you lose weight soap, ward off evil eye soap, overcome fear soap, health soap, have more energy soap and so on.

It smelled strong, but she swore she used all-natural ingredients. She sold it in her shop, The Craft, along with a random smattering of jewelry and greeting cards. It was a book store first, coffee bean and soap store second, then everything else. It was closed today, Monday.

"Let me smell them again," I said. She held out the palm of her hand and I sniffed. "I can only smell the jasmine."

"You need a better nose then," she said.

"I could put Animal on it."

Sure thing, Boss.

39

"Give me your hand." I sniffed. Instantly, the mingled flavors straightened. "Okay. Jasmine, frankincense, sandalwood, lilac—hmmmm—orange peel, nice, and lavender." I looked at her.

"Well done, Animal," she said.

No problem, babe.

"Animal thanks you."

I could do neat little tricks like that. Animal had no clue which scent was which, but I did. He took the nose and I did the translation. One could ask why I don't go around all the time with heightened senses. Truth is, I do a lot. And when you can do it *any* time, you don't have a real desire to do it *all* the time.

"You hungry?"

We sat down in a little Irish pub and drank coffee and water until the blood pudding, bangers and mash arrived. Then we got a Baileys and talked about whether or not Dickens really had made nightly forays into the dark underbelly of London to dig up corpses in order to work out how to dissolve them in quicklime.

"If he did, he was probably so senile he didn't know what he was doing."

"Or who he was," I agreed.

"Maybe he fancied himself one of his characters."

"That would be creepy."

"He was probably just doing research on his book. Which one was it?"

"Edwin Drood," I said.

"Yeah, well, maybe his research was actually committing a murder."

The phone buzzed. It was Walser.

I answered it. "Hey, man."

"Thomas. Hey. So, Radcliffe just signed off on it. We can use you on the case. Why don't you come over tomorrow morning around ten o'clock?"

"I'll be there."

Chapter 4

I drove to 850 Bryant and parked on the street. It had taken me all of three minutes to get there, since I lived around the corner. I leaned up against my car, arms crossed, staring at the multi-storied, cement building. I did not find it beautiful. It was not a work of art or, despite its size, an architectural accomplishment. Pigeons favored it as an enormous, six-storied outhouse.

A cool breeze kept the sun from heating the air. I was wearing a black wool sweater and jeans. I'd dispensed with the beanie and combed my hair. I had to maintain some semblance of decorum, because I came in peace, and I needed a minute to ensure I could make good on that..

I watched two cops shoot the bull on the steps of the great Hall of Justice. I had a lot of friends here, I just didn't remember any of them. And all my enemies held positions of authority. If I have a schtick, that's it: resisting Authority. We don't mix. I couldn't tell you exactly why. And it isn't like I'm some bad-boy rebel. I just have something in me that cannot stand a prick in a suit. Or a uniform.

Pricks in suits hate when guys in beanies tell them what they really think. Well, I would have to keep my opinions to myself for a while, because for that reason alone, those same suits had kicked this beanie wearing fool out of the game—good investigator or not. There are a lot of good investigators who don't come to work anymore. Testaments to the motto: "You are not indispensible no matter how good you think you are."

I crossed the street and skipped up the stairs, ignoring looks from the hard working cops, and got in line at the metal detector.

Those looks. Supposedly I knew these guys. They all thought I had graduated up the food chain and now refused to associate with them. Oh, that's irony for you. When they looked at me, they saw a prick in jeans because the other me—the one that died—used to be a cop.

The unit I work with now doesn't exist in their world—or any world, for that matter.

Even Walser comes and goes in silence. Most just think he's a private attorney. He might have been an officer in Investigations or Homicide if he'd been given a regular job, but Paranormal Interest Crimes exists only in the mind. No trace on paper or electronically.

I suppose we could fit in with Special Victims, since all the victims in these cases are technically "special," but putting our unit alongside rape and domestic violence doesn't really work, despite the occasional crazy who reports dead police officers snooping through his drawers.

There are a handful of private dicks and plainclothes detectives who work with the Paranormal Interest Crimes Unit, such as myself, but they operate on a strictly civilian agenda; they hold no rank or badge.

I took the elevator to the fifth floor and went to room 525.1, inside of which the décor looked like a five-star hotel compared to the drab 1960s yellows and greens everywhere else in the Hall.

"Here to see Walser."

The secretary, who tripled as the private eye's girl Friday slash paranormal CSI tech slash dominatrix (and who always pretended to ignore me) rang his phone.

"Hunter's here, sir…sure thing."

She's pretty. Really pretty. And though I don't usually get oversexed by women, I do with this one. Problem with her—Jessica Rollins-Gray (because she's too proud to completely change her name)—is that she thinks, knows and broadcasts that she's pretty. Beautiful. Hot. Whatever. It's just narcissism. Then again, who I am to cast stones? Why should I care if this chick wants to show off? She isn't hurting the scenery. Either way, I never really want to talk to her, because she's cold and when she laughs it has no joy, at least not for me.

Anyway, I always stared at her ass while she filed police papers.

"Hunter." A voice that was slow, easy and comfortable, said my name like a reverend says a prayer.

"Doug." I walked to him and hugged him. "It's good to see

you."

"Come in. Jess, no calls." He closed the door behind him. "Have a seat." The smell of his office set my nerves to rest. A familiar, rich aroma: good coffee. His office always smelled like that, not because he brewed coffee, but because he stored all types of fair-trade roasts in little brown paper bags.

"You want a cup?"

"No. Doug you don't have to—"

"Oh, no, no. Thomas Hunter sitting in my office is an occasion worthy of celebration. And I remember how much you love a good cup. Am I right? Yeah, look you're already smiling. You just sit tight." He snatched up a bag and poked his head out the door. "Jess, honey, can you make two cups of this? Cream and no sugar, I got that right, Thomas? Hmm? Here you go, sweetie. Thank you. No sugar. Not mine either. Good."

"You are gonna love that one, Thomas." He sat down across the desk from me. "You look good."

"Thanks."

"You feel good? Don't lie. I'll know if you do."

"I'm fine."

He nodded his head amicably. "You see, bullshit. I told you," he said

"I just need to get back to work."

"Too many voices in your head?"

"Oh, no. They don't bother me."

He winked. "And I'm not talking about them. I'm talking about *her*." Somehow or other he always had this effect on me. I guess he must have it on everyone. There is simply no such thing as lying to him. Only the illusion of it. Somehow, I find a great bit of security in that.

I groaned.

"You didn't want to say it, I know. It's okay in here, Hunter. It's okay in your warehouse and its okay in your head. Outside is a different story. You kept the weight off, though."

"You expected me to fatten up, did you?"

"Expected, no. Feared? A little."

"I didn't think you knew me before," I said.

"Before? Before what? I don't know any of those beat cops. And from what you tell me, you weren't even you back then. No, I say that only because I know what can happen not working, lazing round with too much time to drink yourself to death."

A petite knuckle rapped on the door.

"Oh, good. You're gonna love this. Come in!" Jessica entered with a tray, which held two steaming mugs, a tiny stainless steel creamer and a plate of neatly stacked sugar cubes. She wore a most pleasant smile. I admired the way her cleanly manicured fingers worked when she set my cup before me and poured the cream. Not an ounce of hesitation. No motion wasted. Yeah, she was pretty frickin' hot.

"That's good!" But she had already stopped, presumably knowing the exact right amount of milk needed. She did the same for Walser, who just sat there pleasantly waiting for her to finish up. Then, with a pair of tongs, seemingly constructed for this purpose and no other, she picked up one lump of sugar and gently released it into his cup.

"Look at this," said Walser. He gestured toward the sugar cubes. "Utter perfection. Thank you, dear."

Mrs. Jessica Rollins-Gray departed as pleasantly as she had arrived, and then I finally got it. She was cold to me because she didn't need anything else. She got it all from Doug Walser. I don't mean illicitly. I mean professionally. Just like I did, she loved working for this man.

"Take a sip."

"Whoa, that is good. Really good. What are they putting in this, cocaine?"

He smiled in a glow of satisfaction.

"Anyway, Hunter, you don't have to sugarcoat. Anything. Not to me. To everyone else, yes, but not to me. We have a very interesting case on our hands. Very interesting." He was nodding and smiling that thin lipped grin, which meant a great deal of truth lay in that statement. "This may very well prove out to be one of the *most* interesting cases I'll ever work on." He chuckled, mostly to himself. "I say that with a grain of salt. But I gotta know a few things, and then you gotta know a few things, first. Okay?"

"Shoot," I said, setting my cup down.

"You gotta convince me you can play by the rules, at least ninety percent of them. You know what that means, everything by the letter. No entering without a warrant. No roughing up suspects. No lip to the pricks in suits. No disappearing acts in the middle of the case and, Hunter, no—none, absolutely not-at-all—booze. You convince me you can abide by those four things and I can get you on the case. If you think you can't, you just tell me right here over this delicious cup of coffee and no harm no foul, because this case is *that* important."

I nodded. The gravity of his words stung, but I knew he was right, and it was this alone that allowed me to sit there and come to terms with the state of my reputation. I wouldn't be able to come back without Walser, not because some higher up would deny it, but because I myself would prevent it. We both knew that. This man never exaggerated. You knew exactly where you stood, and it was always just as he said it.

"Because the department is *that* upset with me."

He shook his head.

"No. Not the department. Two people in the department. But, Hunter, if either of those two people get wind of any rogue, yahoo bullshit from you, you'll be thrown off this thing just as fast as you can say 'mother fucker.'"

I gathered my thoughts, my intent.

"But you'll know if I lie," I said.

"I will. But if you tell me you can do it, you and I know it's not a statement of fact, but a pledge. With me, Hunter, not with them. Just between you and me."

I was biting my lip. Nothing else existed in the universe but for this moment with this man. Doug Walser, a captain without a badge. The room had gone stone silent. The room and my head.

My Third eye stare had nothing on this. I was a cornered cat in the spotlight. No games in this office. No phony bravado. No finger pointing or blaming. And no self-recrimination. Just truth and sanity.

"And my sources?"

"Don't give a crap," he said. "You can have your sources; keep them as confidential as you want. You can use all the fringe ability and mumbo jumbo you can manage, just don't fuck up in the four points we just went over."

I took a deep breath. "Then, yeah, I can do it."

His face softened into a relaxed smile. "I know."

Time seemed to start up again. "Well good!" he proclaimed. "When you—when we—finish our cups of *Principe Oscuro* here, we'll take a little field trip so that we can bring you up to speed on the case. You should like the sound of that."

"I'm sorry. Our what?"

He gestured to his cup. "Dark Prince."

I took another sip. "Then where?"

"The morgue."

ꓱ ꓕ ꓕ୧

We took the elevator back to the first floor and went out through the covered patio to the Medical Examiner's facilities. The clerk at the front desk, behind the plexiglass, recognized us right away and buzzed us in.

By myself, I would probably have had to lie to gain direct access to the morgue, but Walser had carte blanche. Probably the clerk didn't even know why, letting him in by force of habit.

The green, tile walls of the morgue always reminded me of a 1950s high school shower room, but the piles of stainless steel implements and rows of sink-beds bespoke another purpose entirely. I was glad that no autopsies were underway this morning, though if there had been, I don't think they would have allowed us in, Walser's mysterious all-pass or not.

That "I left the steak in the fridge for two weeks too long" smell permeated the air. I didn't mind it really. The dead stink. It's a fact of life.

We walked past the sinks and the hedge clippers, used for opening chest cavities, to the big live-in refrigerator at the far end.

"Right here." We stopped before a gurney.

I noticed my heart beating. Was I nervous? No, couldn't be. Excited maybe. Then I realized: I had absolutely no idea what he was going to show me. He had said this might prove to be one of the most interesting cases he had ever worked on. Was that even possible coming from Walser, who'd seen more than a lifetime of the paranormal?

"You ready?" Walser stood over it as if he might perform a trick.

I shrugged. "What's under there?"

He smiled. "I could tell you, but you would never believe me. Best to show you." And with that he pulled off the sheet.

I was not impressed, only a little confused. Walser finished with the sheet and gathered it up on the counter.

"Isn't he handsome?"

I had to agree. Handsome as he would have been in life. In fact, he scarcely looked dead.

"Go ahead. Touch him." Walser was pressing a hand against the cadaver's shoulder.

"What is he, still warm?" I touched the shoulder and met with a cold bit of flesh. I touched the chest, same thing. "Room temp."

"Mmhhmm. Now, Hunter, this is a test. What do you notice about this corpse?"

"With or without Third?" I asked.

He shrugged. "Either way."

I inspected first with my live vision.

"Well, I see the relatively good-looking body of a gentlemen in his late thirties. Remarkably fit, waxed chest, average sized…penis. A large frame, a little shorter than myself but—ah, yeah, he's been working out and eating right."

"Continue."

I was squinting trying to guess at the catch.

"Third, give me what you got, por favor."

"Come on, Hunter, just look and tell me what you see."

Third clicked on and I shut my live eye. The body lay there in cold, grainy shadows. Nothing else, not even an aura. This guy was dead for sure, but not dead. I've seen that kind of thing before, but then the dead guy had been moving around, doing things. And even the undead have an aura if you know where to look.

"Hunter, time's up."

I opened my live eye and Third faded out.

"He doesn't look dead," I said. "Or if he is, he's no more than an hour old, but then he's cold as ice and has no aura at all, so he's been dead a while, longer than an hour, maybe three. Spiritually, maybe a day or two, but then he's got no lividity—either front or posterior—and no scent and—" I took the hand, lifted and dropped it. It flopped onto the bed just as flaccid as if he were sleeping. I looked at Walser. "What the fuck, Doug?"

"I'm sorry, is that part of your official report?"

"No rigor mortis. Should I be checking for a pulse on this guy?"

"Go for it. Pulse. Heart beat. Breath. Pupil dilation. How long you reckon he's been dead? Your official opinion, of course."

I laughed a short, wry chortle. "Like I said, *if* he's dead, maybe three hours. I guess. It's all just a guess."

"Try three weeks."

I shook my head and inhaled. "Not possible."

"Three weeks, Hunter. Three weeks that we can say for certain. Probably more like four since he went missing from his day job."

I just stood and shook my head. Then stopped and looked at Walser. This was no joke. This was Walser. We were standing in a morgue. A naked, dead body lay on the table between us.

"You're not kidding," I said, a statement.

He shook his head. "Nope."

Finally, I said, "How?"

Monday, August 6ᵗʰ
Office of the Medical Examiner
San Francisco, CA
10:45 a.m.

The body arrives clothed in a bathrobe and pajama bottoms.

The vestments are removed and the body is viewed unclothed. The body is that of a normally developed Caucasian male appearing between 35 and 40 years of age, measuring 72 inches in height and weighing 190 lbs. There is typical male pattern hair growth about the chest, pubis and limbs...

"Skip to the good parts. Here, start with this paragraph."

> I am informed at the time of
> viewing that the body is believed to
> have been deceased for a period of
> roughly one week. I see no evidence
> of putrefaction, either visually or
> olfactorily on any aspect of the
> body. To the contrary, the scent of
> the body is sweet. I find no evidence
> of advanced lividity, no evidence
> of pallor mortis, no cyanosis, no
> rigor mortis, no algor mortis, and
> no pulse.

The report went on to describe taking the pulse from different locations, flicking the eyelids and tapping nerve centers, all of which yielded no results. The examiner had also drawn blood and confirmed that no one had come along and pumped the corpse full of embalming fluids. Then came the line that just creeped me out:

> I observe a light layer of perspiration
> on the forehead and upper lip.

The examiner had died of a massive heart attack two days after he'd written it.

"Toxicology yielded nothing out of the ordinary," said Walser. "Then the Vatican called and laid claim."

"The *Vatican?*"

He nodded. "They call them Incorruptibles. Ever hear of them?"

"Folks who don't decompose after dying? Is this guy a saint or something?"

"Brian Matthew Johnston," Walser said crossing his arms and staring down at the body. "Age thirty-six. Worked as a network manager for a big hedge fund company downtown. Made about two hundred K a year. Single. Ate vegan and smoked pot, but not cigarettes. Didn't like beer but had a soft spot for Japanese rice wine. Japanese women, too, judging by his porn collection."

"Devout Catholic on the side?"

"Only if you are."

"I don't get it. Why won't the Vatican lay off?"

He shrugged. "They're not convinced. Apparently they have evidence to show otherwise. I don't believe it. The man was no more Catholic than Crowley, but the Vatican has some claim on things considered to be Holy Relics."

Interesting choice of words. "So, how did he die?"

"That's just it, Hunter. We found him in his car. In the garage, with a vacuum hose hooked from the exhaust pipe into the window."

"A bit old school, eh?"

"With half a tank of gas."

"Right," I said. "Dead guy turned off the car to save on gas money."

Walser continued, "California and now, thank God, Washington isn't releasing the body. And we don't have a media leak on the thing—yet—so here we sit with our thumbs up our asses."

I shook my head. "I don't get it. He's dead but he's not. And he's not undead."

Walser leaned forward. "Hunter, we may not be able to cut into this guy, but we've done everything else. X-rays, ultra sounds, CTs. There is nothing keeping this guy from getting up and going to work. Except for being clinically dead. It's like the clock just stopped ticking for this guy. He's more preserved than Will Rogers."

"You said he made good money. Does it lead anywhere?"

He shook his head. "Nah, too young for a legacy."

"Clubs? Associations?"

"Yeah. He was a member of Triple A. I'm telling you, Hunter, we've looked. No secret cabals, no magick shit. He's clean. Even his porn is rated PG."

I nodded. "What else?"

He crossed his arms and stared back at me with a squint. "There's another one."

He turned around and pointed to another gurney. This time I noticed the feet weren't black and blue.

"Brace yourself for this one, Hunter."

He unveiled it.

"I see what you mean."

Walser filled me in on the details: Elizabeth Link Schneider from Sunland, California. Age twenty-five with one fine looking physique. Tan, blonde with small but shapely breasts. Lying there she looked like a woman about to get implants. Unconscious. She simply did not look dead. She'd worked at World's Gym, but nothing too remarkable about Elizabeth Link Schneider from Sunland, California aside from her nudity.

She'd divorced her husband to go lesbo. Otherwise, no drugs, no booze. Nothing.

"Catholic?"

He shook his head. "Buddhist."

"Parents?"

"Lutherans from the Midwest," he sighed. "Not a Catholic bone in the family. What I find weird about Link Schneider," said Walser as he pulled the cloth over the girl, "is not so much that she doesn't decompose—as if that's not odd enough—but LA Robbery Homicide contacted *us*. Said the Vatican called *them* and wanted her shipped *here*."

"So who's tipping the pope off?"

"Good question. Meanwhile, here we are babysitting the two of them. Johnston the unassuming playboy and Link Schneider the beautiful lesbian. Nothing to tie them together."

"Are we talking to the Vatican?"

He chuckled. "Yeah, I just ring up old Pope Francis and play a game of twenty questions."

"Hhmm. So, how was Link Schneider found?"

"Girlfriend came home after a business trip and found her on the couch with an empty bottle of Xanax."

"And?"

"Her blood test doesn't show a thing."

I nodded. "Two suicides—both who didn't go through with their plan but died anyway. How long was she lying there?"

"Four or five days. The meal she was eating got moldy. Their coroner reacted the same way as ours did—total 'what the fuck.'"

"Any notes left behind?"

"Him? No. She left a little love letter to her girlfriend saying she'd love her forever or some such."

I laughed. "So what do you make of it?"

"These two are either fuck ups or plants."

I raised an inquisitive eyebrow.

"Meaning, someone either wanted us to find them or got sloppy and then tipped off the Vatican to cover their tracks."

"You think there's more of these Incorruptibles out there?"

He looked at me for a moment. "Something tells me yes."

Chapter 5

I left feeling perplexed. And intrigued. Of course my mind was spiraling. I kept recalling the images of Brian and Elizabeth on their gurneys. Had Walser not informed me otherwise, I would have thought they were sleeping. I thought of the medical examiner, who had begun a report he would never complete. And his body *had* gone through all the stages of mortis and decay and now lay with the roots of oak trees, sheltered from the airborne shit of sparrows.

I worked the streets like an Olympic slalom and ended up on 25th Avenue. Took that as a straight shot up to China Beach, where things get pretty. And foggy. I squashed out my second cigarette and stepped from my car. The air here makes me happy. I inhaled. Fresh eucalyptus, clean and wholesome, and yet the whole neighborhood looked too damn perfect. Nothing's this perfect.

Brian Johnston's condo had police tape over the door. I stripped it away, slid the key into the latch and entered.

Nice place. Lamentably, the floors had allowed themselves to be carpeted, but the carpet was new and clean, and I really couldn't complain, despite my penchant for hardwood. Deep sage and fire-engine red gave the place some depth. The sigil of the I Ching, painted on an entire wall in the living room, was a nice touch. Classy for a white guy. Everything had its place; there was no clutter. Men's fitness magazines and like paraphernalia were stacked in neat piles. What I expected. Everything just like I expected. Outside and in. I didn't like it.

"Does a man live here, Boss? Cuz it smells like a woman."

"He must have been a fop," I said.

"What's that?"

"A good looking and really well-dressed—forget it. Third, hi, please click on…er, whatever you do to make my eye go."

She did.

As for Brian Johnston's condo—and life—I just didn't believe this immaculate perfection. Japanese porn? I found his collection. Erotic art house books and magazines with pretty Japanese girls sitting naked in the middle of bamboo forests. Come on! All neatly stacked on a lacquered, driftwood shelf for anyone to see? That's not porn. That's cover up.

I searched the place with Third, starting in the living room and then the kitchen, the two bathrooms, the bedroom and his office. I didn't find anything out of the ordinary. No energies. No overlays. Just regular old pictures of guys and girls hugging Johnston at parties. I sat down on the couch and stared at the blank television screen. Then I sat back like I lived there. Not bad digs. I could do some damage here. I got up and went back into the bedroom. The bed didn't look slept in.

Well, I had checked the name on the mail kiosk and opened the door with his key. Then it hit me. I went back into the closet, a nice big rambler you could take a hike in, and went to the empty spot in the middle of the expensive shoe collection. I looked up.

"Bingo."

A man-sized square made an outline in the ceiling. I reached up, pulled out the recessed lever then tugged. The panel gave way to an accordion ladder.

"Boss, you always find the hidden spots."

"You're damn right I do."

I climbed up into darkness. Darkness is darkness for both eyes. I didn't have a flashlight, but I did have a lighter. I used it to find a light switch.

Red, diffused neon showed me a store of leather in all shapes, but only one color.

"Score," I whispered, creeping through like I'd entered the temple of the Holy Grail. He wasn't here, his ghost. No presences, just a lot of well thought out industry. He'd put some time and money into this special nook. Dark, glossy wood made the floor, under an A-frame truss with no windows. He hadn't wanted anyone seeing in or out. There was also a Saint Andrew's Cross on the far wall, apple red of course ("Naughty, naughty"), a bench with belts and other apparatuses I couldn't decide the use of, a rack of tools, whips and chains and little paddles not made for row boats or horseback riding, balls with straps, handcuffs and doggie collars.

"What have you been doing up here, Brian?" Then I spotted the long, spiky ones. "Or should I say 'who?'"

It was then that I noticed the mural, expertly rendered, but in an off-white paint.

"Oh, here we go."

I flicked off the light and, sure enough, the wall-sized drawing glowed. The Eye of Horus, that all-seeing peeper of the Illuminati. And there was one more item. Under the mural sat the old party gag itself: a Ouija board.

Through Third, a wan phosphorescent light shone off it. Not glow paint, but the real thing. I didn't take the board. I didn't have to. I left and sealed it all back up like I'd never come.

He hadn't just dropped dead or gone into an Incorruptible coma. He'd invited it. One way or another, he'd asked for it.

Time to jet. The Box had been waiting patiently, for which I thanked it. Then I split. Golden Gate Bridge was a quick jaunt from the China Beach neighborhood, and after I paid the toll, I sort of didn't care how long it took to get to my destination.

I couldn't go snooping around Elizabeth's abode, because her lover lived there. If she knew anything about occult connections, she wasn't likely to tell me anyway.

Sausalito sat like a jewel on the California coast. I stopped on the waterfront and stepped amidst the afternoon leisure class into a coffee shop. No sugar, an inch of half and half. Two girls with lavishly brushed, brown hair and riding boots sat at one table, sipping lattes and discussing something important.

These highborn ladies did not pay an ounce of attention to me. I liked that about this town. You didn't have to be there to be there. No one would ever know or care that you had come and partaken in their overpriced horse and dog society. These women were pretty under their makeup, prettier maybe. I liked their clothes. I liked their hands and I liked their soft spoken words. It seemed better that way. Private. The city liked to invade your senses. Marin County liked to block you out. I think you need both to stay sane.

On my way out, I idled through town then hit a small highway.

After ten minutes, I pulled down a dirt road. The house sat tucked way in the back of the property, and you couldn't see it from the road. You would never have known anything was even there until you got to the enormous, arched, iron gates and the huge, cement wall that traveled out to either side and around the whole property. Two weathered gargoyle statues guarded either side.

"Hello, boys," I said. "Looking stoned as usual."

I buzzed the intercom while staring up into the micro camera.

The metal box beeped and the doors began a steady parting. I had never known Dax not to be home, and I had never known him to answer his phone. It was only the intercom. Always the intercom. To be sure, he left his country citadel at times, but they were never at times when I would normally come. Dax was so reclusive that he ordered all his necessary services via proxy. Few folks in town had ever even seen him. The house was not listed under any of the various names Dax went by, including Dax, but rather under the name of a front company, Greenville Realty LTD.

I ambled down the overgrown dirt path, under a canopy of equally overgrown cypress and wild flowers. Dax kept the drive purposely wild. On occasion, curious nosey parkers outwitted the hidden camera and scaled the walls, landing on the other side amidst the weeds and unkempt flora. If they managed to locate the path and follow it all the way up, God help them.

I pulled up to the welcoming party, a pack of Doberman pinschers. I eyed them from inside my car. I had no idea which dogs were which so could not call them by name. This was no ordinary home, and the way in to it was through these well-trained and extremely loyal beasts. You just had to trust their canine memories.

The house looked no different. It was huge, a brownstone affair with too many windows and a wide front porch that Dax never used, favoring as he did the servants' entrance. It had been an old mill house originally.

I opened my car door and let the first nose find my crotch. The animal sniffed gruffly.

Animal: *Hold on, Boss, let me get things ready!*
Me: *We're not going to fight them.*
Animal: *Huh?*

Me: *We're not going to fight Dax's guard dogs.*
Animal: *We can take 'em, Boss, just give me a second—*
Me: *Animal, knock it off. Be very still.*

Still. I felt Animal and Kairos do their thing and galvanize my body starting with my most sensitive parts, since that's where the Doberman was sniffing. Oh, galvanizing that part is not what you might think, the opposite actually, which is kind of embarrassing but far more effective.

When the dog finished he backed off, sat down and barked, wagging his tail. This was the signal. He'd given me the all clear, so I got out and let the others circle around me and jump up on me and wag their tales and slobber until the door opened.

There stood a broad-shouldered man, six foot six, with olive skin and shoulder-length, black ringlets. He wore a single multi-colored cloth around his waist. He had over a dozen earrings, which I doubted he ever took off. He was fit. I guessed he weighed no more than two hundred pounds, which meant about sixteen percent body fat. He wore no shoes. I could smell his rich, lavender oils. The man was very fond of such scents. I hugged him.

"Been a while, Hunter." He was smiling handsomely, a mouth full of healthy teeth.

"I know. I'm back in business. And I need your advice."

"Come in."

I followed Dax inside. I could smell the smoky perfume of his incense. He burned it constantly. Dax didn't smoke, but he loved smoke.

We walked down a narrow corridor before entering the main foyer. The Old World design made me feel giddy inside. Marble floors, a vaulted ceiling with gilded patterns, two huge stairways on either side of the entrance and something new: a macabre statue of Theseus slaying the Minotaur.

Dax walked past all of this, naturally uninterested, but I took a moment to examine the artwork. I always did when I came here, because he always seemed to have something new and not from junkyard sales, either. The man moved in higher circles.

The stone, I observed, was alabaster. I wondered which museum he'd bought it from. It was not unlike Dax to purchase such things from Italy, Crete, Tanzania, or New York.

I moved on. Dax was sitting on a bed of messily arranged silk cushions while a pile of perfumed wood smoked up the living room.

"Hey, Hunter." Ellen Hart was eyeing me from behind the open refrigerator door. Aside from a pair of white panties, she was naked. Her breasts were small. They looked like little pears with nipples. I could see the outline of her spine and ribs. She was a dirty blonde, cute, sensual and way too skinny. Two glistening puncture wounds stared at me from her neck, dripping just a little.

She plucked a glass bottle of dark red liquid from the refrigerator. I wondered if it was claret.

"Haven't seen you in a while," she said and came over to give me a hug. I always noticed the sandy patches under her arms. Hippy chicks and German girls never seem to shave their pits. She smelled feral. Unwashed. I hugged her. It felt good to hold someone so thin in my arms. Made me feel huge, and she fit there easily.

"I've been on vacation," I said.

"Oh, don't you mean unemployed?"

"Same thing."

"You're cute," she said, grabbed a wine glass and slunk off toward her silk cushions. I was staring at her ass, assessing the fat to muscle ratio, when something caught my eye. Once it did, it wouldn't let go. It was hairy and disturbing and mounted on the other side of the room.

"Dax, you never bore do you?" I walked over to examine it more closely.

"You like that, Hunter?"

"I do," I said. "You killed this thing?"

"Not personally," he said, "Lucy is an heirloom."

I jerked my thumb. "It's a female?"

Dax chuckled. "Lucy as in Lucifer. It's what my kind called their enemies. Kind of like calling a Viet Cong 'Charlie.'"

"You get it from the same place you got the Minotaur?"

"Hardly."

"It's amazing." It leered down at me—just a head, huge and properly stuffed no doubt. On second thought, probably not. Nevertheless, it had a neck as stout as a tree limb, a wild mane of brown fur. The maw gaped open at least a foot and a half with porcelain white fangs. And the eyes, my God, those eyes. I wondered if it was a trick of the preserving art and then thought better of it. No, those eyes could never be tame…or kind.

"That's one fuck of a werewolf," I said.

"Wolf-therian," Dax corrected.

"Oh, right. Wouldn't want to confuse terms."

I was sitting in front of Dax and Ellen. Both were drinking a particularly red, nearly black, drink. Both eyed me with some amusement. Dax hoisted the bottle at me.

"No."

"Its wine," he assured me and poured me a glass, while Ellen pulled out two cigarettes, lit them, and handed me one.

"It's been a long time, Hunter. What have you been doing?" Dax asked.

"Dying of boredom mainly."

"Ghosts?" asked Ellen.

"Yeah, ghosts. Pretentious, trust-fund-baby ghosts."

"Aren't you a trust-fund baby?"

I shrugged. "Yes. But I'm not pretentious."

"But now you're on a case?" Dax took a drink of his wine. I watched a thin residue slide down the crystal of his cup. Mine didn't do that.

"Yeah. Well, I needed to do something more, shall we say, intriguing." I took a drag of my cigarette.

"Walser put you on something hot?"

I nodded slowly. Dax knew about my professional life. He was one of my sources. I used him mainly as a sort of living library and expert advisor. I told him about what I'd seen in the morgue. I told him the stories of Handsome Brian and Sexy Elizabeth and how Walser thought they had been planted. He brooded over all this, took a long gulp of his drink and solemnly said, "Huh."

"Thanks for your expert advice," I said.

Ellen found this ridiculously funny and slapped Dax across the shoulder.

"Dax!"

He smiled in spite of himself. "Therianthropic."

59

I didn't say anything as I observed him, deep in thought. He looked extremely handsome at that moment. Something about the far off cast of his eyes that brought out the rich, Arabian heritage. Finally, he broke reverie.

"Those bodies. They are therianthropic in nature."

I blew out a taupe cloud. "Shape shifting?"

"The first and major clue to therianism is the body doesn't decompose, so these Incorruptible bodies have that in common with therians, that's all I'm saying. Beyond that, who knows.

"Shape shifting or therianism or what some call the Otherkin, is obviously far more advanced than that, but the moment we begin talking about this, we get into current fads, which is why I hate— fucking hate—to use those words. But then you don't understand me if I don't, so I have no choice." He leaned forward, instructive.

"They call it 'undead,' without a clue as to what that word really means. It's a body undergoing constant shape shifting—aka becoming therian. It's noted by a constant change from one form to another. Actually, the body is fossilizing.

"Take me for instance. I'm almost a millennia old and by all rights, I should be a stone statue by now, except that being therian means I am constantly changing back to the first form I held: a man. So, I'm a man-therian, or what the vernacular calls a 'vampire.'

"The bones are the first to go and with them, the red blood cells, which is why we therians have to drink blood no matter which form we take."

I sat back and smoked. I was trying to get used to this idea of therianism being little more than some kind of bizarre bone marrow cancer.

Dax continued. "Anyways, we're always dying, which is where you get the 'un' in dead. Meaning 'not dead,' yet the death is drawn out, happening forever."

"So, an undead is always dying slowly, so then he never completely dies?" I asked.

Dax nodded. "And that's the paradox. Always dying, never dead. Thus we say 'un-dead.' I like to say 'fossilizing' because that is precisely what an undead is—an animated fossil. But," he shrugged, "we don't want to confuse it with archeology, either."

"Wait, so, undead means 'not dead at all?'" I asked.

"Yeah, that's what I said, Hunter."

"Because I used to think it meant like dead and animated, or a walking corpse or something."

Dax sighed. "I know. God, I know. Because you've watched too many modern movies. It means exactly what it says. 'Un,' as in 'not' dead because obviously—just look at me—we don't die."

"Right," I said. "You fossilize. Forever."

"Getting smarter by the minute, Hunter."

"Okay, so what?"

"So, let me explain a bit of our history." He pointed to the werewolf head on the wall. "Take Lucy over there. He's an enemy of my people, but 'before the enemy exists the brother.' Meaning the wolf-therian, or lycanthrope, or werewolf, is first a therian regardless of breed. People like me" —he gritted his teeth— "a fucking vampire—God, I hate those terms, Hunter!—are no different. In the beginning we were all just shape shifters.

"The bloodline became diversified and then set, so that now we're considered different races, but that's ignorance.

"Like mankind, therians make different races within the big race. Some became wolves, or wolf-like, others stayed men, or man-like. There are others, as well, but those are the two big ones."

"Anyway, at the root of all this, and what I am getting at in terms of your case, is the same basic building block and a body that does not decay—in a traditional sense. So, you see the lack of decay is a kind of shape shifting in itself. Shifting from one substance to another all the time. Flesh and blood putrefy. The corpse of a man breaks down and returns to its chemical compounds. That's known science. Flesh and blood that is undead or fossilizing does not. It's the first shift of shape, if you will. Cellular change."

"And the next change?"

He shrugged. "Man, wolf, bat, whatever. The list is infinite. It doesn't even matter. It's just changing. Shifting. Call it the current fashion if you want. Preferred pedigree. You would think that man-therian is easier to maintain than say, wolf, but I don't know that that's true at all. I like man-therian because I like my original body."

"Can you forget how to go back?" I asked.

He nodded. "Just like with anything else, you get rusty, but with this you also get stuck. Then, it's just what you're used to, what you know how to be—or in the case of most shape shifters, what your ancestors learned for you. I know there are wolf-therians who don't know themselves as anything other than wolves. They're completely stuck. DNA wise it's all the same. Anyway, your Incorruptables are changing, because they have to in order to maintain an appearance of no change, because the elements and gravity are working on them all the time."

"But they don't drink blood," I said.

"Right, which is why I said 'therianthropic in nature.'"

I sat back and thought it over. "Then there must be a different medium than blood that can sustain the change."

Dax shrugged. "Obviously. Since your Incorrputibles aren't waking up in the middle of the night and drinking blood. At least we don't think."

"I hope not."

He shrugged it off. "Not likely. Have you tried viewing the body through Third?"

I nodded.

"And?"

"Nothing."

"With Third under a microscope?"

"Hadn't thought of it," I said, honestly.

"Try it. You may see something in the cells. I would think, anyway. Somehow they have to stay hydrated. Hunter, those things could easily reanimate if what you say is true. They're being preserved for a purpose."

"I agree," I replied, but something else was nagging me in the back of my mind. "Does that mean I'm undead?"

He laughed. "Oh, Hunter. You're a funny mother fucker."

"Well, I did die. And for more than two minutes."

"How long did they say?"

"Twenty minutes or something."

Dax shrugged. "That's a long time to be dead for flesh and blood, I agree. But you're not undead, from what I can see. Though I could be wrong."

"Therian maybe?"

"Yeah…maybe. Honestly, I've never figured out what you are. You're something new under the sun. You're not fossilizing, at least from what I can tell."

"Why?"

"You don't need to drink blood."

"It's that simple?"

"All therians have to drink blood. Have to."

Dax had taught me a lot of things but never what I was. He was mostly concerned about what he was, and I suppose that made sense.

"Though," he said, sitting up and gesturing to Ellen, "you could try it."

Ellen looked at me. No, her eyes bored in to me. Suddenly, a side of her that I had not experienced came leaping out. It made my heart tick noticeably and my cheeks flush. That feeling you get when a woman stares you down across a room. Heady.

Then it occurred to me: she wanted me to drink her blood. The casual permission from her lover had ignited the nascent spark of passion, of blood lust. It took an almost palpable characteristic across the pillows and smoke. The image of it burst into my mind. Taking her into my arms, putting my lips to those open wounds and letting the blood flow onto my tongue. Then pulling off her thin panties and making love to her. The impulse demanded taking her right here and now. She had slunk forward already, stalking across the pillows on hands and knees.

I felt my body drawn to hers. She was going to crawl into my arms, and I was going to take her right now. Dax would not stop it. Dax would not care. Because Ellen was simply one of several. *I have never killed for human blood,* Dax had once said, *they always give it freely.* The fantasy was happening.

Boss, don't!

I stopped. Animal advising against a sexual encounter? That was a first. That was unprecedented.

"Wait," I said and put up a hand. "Why?"

"Not right," said Animal.

"Since when are you a moralist?"

"Please, Boss, don't do that. Sex her if you want, but don't drink her. Please."

Well, I knew one did not come without the other. Not in this case. The sexual zeal came from the prospect of drinking. The simple idea that she could give herself up to another therian, or at least someone who might be therian, had ignited her adoration just as fast as Dax had said it. It was a kind of worship therian lovers bestowed on their chosen patron.

But that Animal had reacted so strongly told me there was something else going on here. It made me far more curious than Ellen's sloe-eyed stare.

"Maybe later," I said finally. It was time to go. Ellen backed down, lit another cigarette and stared at her crossed legs. I got up.

"I'm sorry," said Dax. "It was inappropriate."

"No. Forget it. It's fine. I'll figure it out sooner or later."

Dax stood up and walked me out. The dogs were lying in a pile and didn't bother to get up.

"Check on the use of Third under a microscope," he said.

"I will."

"Let me know what you find." He hugged me. "You're always welcome here, Hunter."

"Thanks. Look, if I do want to try out the, uh, blood thing?"

"Any time. She'll be fine in an hour. We got her hopes up is all. But if you do, let me know first, then I can arrange things better, more private and whatnot."

I wondered how I would let him know beforehand since he didn't have a phone. I guessed he expected me to use the intercom exclusively.

"Can I ask why you decided against it?"

"Animal says 'no,' and I don't know why. He must have a good reason, though sometimes his reasoning isn't all that sane. I just need to look into it a bit more," I said.

"Sure thing."

Truth be told I had no idea what drinking Ellen's blood would do, other than open up a lusty sexual episode. I felt bad on my drive back to the city. I was thinking of Eva. I felt like I had somehow just cheated on her.

Still, the prospect of finding out what the blood might do inside me was very alluring. It could have something to do with the case, though I couldn't substantiate that yet. I felt like I was just making excuses so I could get laid.

I don't know why I was so hung up on that, but I was. I felt that if I gave in to every sexual craving, I would never stop. If I let Animal go, he would go, let me tell you.

Well, we didn't talk about it. He stayed quiet, and I drove back to Bluxome, back to my warehouse, where I smoked cigarettes and drank espresso and thought about what Dax had said.

Somewhere around three a.m. I answered Eva's text.

`Sry I didn't answer. Busy on this case. I'll call you later.`

She didn't answer. I hadn't expected her to. I pulled out a bottle of Wild Turkey and unscrewed the cap. I heard Walser's voice in my memory and put the cap back on.

My fingers and thumb were pressing together as though holding a pen.

"Not tonight," I said. And I meant it. The twitching stopped.

I thought about surfing the net, but knew I would just look at porn. So I took off my clothes, got into bed and opened up to the next chapter of *Les Miserables*.

I fell asleep before the second paragraph.

Chapter 6

The ME gave me a blood sample, taken from Brian Johnston, and set me up on a big microscope that looked like it would send your electric bill into the triple digits. Once they'd adjusted the slide and helped me adjust the resolution, I put my dead eye to the lens.

"Okay, Third," I whispered. "Show me the goods. Please."

Third switched on. No change.

"Third, come on," I said in a low voice. "Pretty please with... agave." I knew the techs in the lab could hear me and I was trying hard not to sound like a total nut job.

After a bit, an image flashed up, a blank computer screen that read VOID TRANSACTION.

I backed away from the microscope.

"We tried."

5707

I stared at Walser in silence. Animal and Kronos had my whole system galvanized. If my hand was going to go through Walser's wall, they wanted to make sure I would walk away uninjured. My head seemed to want to shake back and forth on its own, perpetually saying 'no.' My jaw clenched and released and my eyes glared fiercely at the man I had once chosen as my mentor.

"This is bullshit." I nearly spat. That's all I had said for the last fifteen minutes.

"Hunter, listen to me." He leaned forward, pushing his cup of fresh brewed Caballo Negro aside. "We feel that you hold the link to this Incorruptible shit, because you came back with no systemic brain damage. No lasting injury. Nothing. Look at you. You're in better shape than ever."

"Yeah, that's why the fuck heads in charge of this department think I'm a schizophrenic nut case, hearing voices and talking to myself, right? Because I'm in such great shape?"

"You say department, but it's one person, Hunter. One person who has to find a reason not to like you for your cowboy attitude. You know that, come on."

"And who's that?"

"Hunter…"

"Who?"

He sighed and sat back. "White. There, now I said it, are you happy? Damn it, Hunter, what difference does it make?"

"Ah, why am I not surprised? Sergeant Greg White, the king of the pricks. The same White prick that's in charge of this investigation, who wants to hook me up to a handful of electrodes and study my brain waves. I wanted a case, Doug. For me to work on! Not to be the lab rat!"

"Settle down, will ya? I got no leads here, Hunter. None. We've been looking for a month now and come up short. You know as well as I do that something like this has roots. Two bodies show up that refuse to decompose. Now, I've simply got to do all that I can to find a way to go here. You're an obvious first choice. Nobody said anything about taking you off the case. It's not like that. They just want to put you under and ask you some questions. See if they can't find something that makes sense."

"You make it sound so easy," I said, "just open me up and out pop the clues. Well, I don't know if there are any in there. I've looked. A lot."

"Hunter, hey," he leaned across the desk, "we both want the same thing here. We want some answers and maybe some leads, and you want your memory back. I think the two things could be one and the same."

"Fuuuuck," I said, more to myself than to him.

"At the very least we find nothing, just like you said. But maybe we find something and maybe you get some of your memory back. Think about it, Hunter. Your memory."

He knew he had me now.

△╟⋉ꝉ

"Special Vic, really? Was I abused?"

"Oh, Hunter, it's just where we could find space to set up." Walser led me through a side door to a much larger room, the purpose of which was dubious. A cot and a metal table graced the far end, where the doctor and the transcriptionist sat quietly.

It felt clinical and cold, and I suddenly had my doubts about doing this.

The doctor wore a stupid, white smock like all trusted practitioners of medicine and the mind, which did anything but put me at ease.

The transcriptionist, my last minute request so that I might have a full record of my own, was a young thing. She was wearing the clothes of her grandmother, which gave no hint of anything. I conceded this was for the best, because I didn't need the distraction.

The doctor smiled big, gestured to the cot. His sincerity was questionable.

I lay down, my hands sweating. The idea of the procedure didn't scare me, but the potential outcome did. And then there was the possibility that I might actually remember and the possibility that I might not. I feared both.

Boss, you gonna let them monkey around under the hood?

Chill out. Nothing's going to happen that we don't want.

Walser sat down backwards on a chair in the far corner, a silent and solemn look in his eyes. A small, handheld, digital tape recorder—not at all like in the movies—was on the table.

The doctor sat down. I could smell his aftershave. Somehow *that* eased me.

"Will you take off your shirt, Mr. Hunter?"

I did. Then he took my arm and rubbed it up and down.

"Now, just relax. Just relax. Don't look here, there's nothing for you to see here. Now, there you go, son, there you go."

I felt the needle jab, but by the time Animal had begun to bellow "Boss is under attack!" he was already being drowned out: the bliss of sodium amytal.

What a wonder drug. I kept thinking that. My crew just seemed to fall away. Not forever, I knew that, but for now. Animal snoozed deeply inside. Third cut out like the severing of an electric cable.

Kairos-Kronos sank into the recesses of my mind, still ticking and calculating, but as unnoticeable as a heartbeat.

It struck me how vulnerable I suddenly was, but at the moment I didn't care. I simply enjoyed the silence.

"You here now, Mr. Hunter, you here?" I heard the doctor saying. I stared at him. He was a small man, short, round about the belly, with a thin white beard and kind eyes. I did not fear him now. Walser. Old Walser sat behind him, and it all just made me happy.

"You here, son?"

"Yup."

"Very good. Now, we're going to do a little looking around. You okay with that?"

"Yup."

"Very good. Now, I want you to go back, way back, as far back as you can remember. I want you to go back and remember what you forgot. Can you do that for me? Can you?"

I went back. The exterior world faded. Nothing there was important to me now. I drifted back, remembering Eva, her sweet smile and her soap. And ghosts, so many ghosts.

Then I punched through to the first year and then the first three months after the accident. The family lawyer, Mr. What's His Name, telling me I was rich for life. Signing papers with a strange name, lying in a hospital bed wondering what it was all about.

Two weeks later the hospital released me. Said it was a miracle. Still, I could not walk. I declined hospice and requested to be delivered to the warehouse on Bluxome.

I found a mattress and blankets, a razor, shaving cream and expensive clothes and shoes no squatter or vagrant could afford. Someone had been using this abandoned place as a safe house or some kind of sleazy, one-room hotel.

And there was another thing too: an early 90s black Porsche Boxter in the garage, tank half full.

I called a locksmith and ordered a pizza.

I slept on the floor, because I didn't trust the mattress. Next day I ordered a bed and a chair and a couch. I had them delivered. Then I called a whore.

She came, wearing a slinky dress and no underwear. Her body

jiggled beneath her clothes. She felt sorry for me and went out to buy sheets. She came back with a bottle of whiskey and a blonde wig, just like I'd asked. She undressed me first and helped me into bed. She unzipped her dress and let it fall to her feet. Then we fucked.

We snorted cocaine between orgasms. Her wig fell off, and I made her put it back on. She was there for two days before she had to report to her pimp. When I came down, after she was gone, I cried. When it passed, I got to work. Ordered more supplies and watched them pile up. Ordered food and toilet paper and whiskey. I drank and started ripping up the laminate floor. I worked on my knees. I worked shirtless and sweaty and drunk. I pulled flooring out by the truck load. I heaped piles of debris by the door. I didn't leave for days. I worked until the bottles ran dry, and then They came.

Voices. Entities. Visions.

At first I was entertained, then horrified. *Who am I? Where am I? How did I get here? What are these voices in my head?*

Who's head, Boss?

But I could walk again.

I could walk and jump and…*how is this possible?*

What about this patch on my eye? Maybe that will come off, too.

But, oh, that was delicate business.

The eye isn't like a leg or an arm. No sir, an eye is—well, a different sort of organ and not very likely—actually damn near impossible to heal. Well, a glass eye can be very convincing nonetheless. And handsome, too.

The voices argued. With themselves, with me. I talked to myself for hours. I watched images float by, faces I didn't know, places I had never been.

But still came the lonely nights, drinking and sobbing, grieving for a life I'd lost, but couldn't remember.

A ghost child came to comfort me. She smiled beautifully under her freckles, in the darkness of my warehouse room. Stood beside my bed until I awoke, staring into her pale blue eyes. She was so solid, so opaque, I thought her real. I could see the individual strands of hair, the detail of her retinas, her eyelashes.

My God, she's an angel.

"It will be okay, Thomas Hunter. I know it, and now so do you.

71

Trust me. Now sleep and heal," she said and vanished.

After that, I remembered Her. A blonde woman. Not the whore I'd made dress up, but one I loved and missed with all my heart. How could I miss someone I didn't even know? But this was the link to my past, wasn't it? The one image that came to my mind that I could feel. It became an obsession.

I called for a true blonde. Her eyes filled with terror at the sight of my home, but relaxed when she came into my room with its new furnishings, area rugs and bed.

"Oh, you're not a creepy serial killer after all."

"Don't talk. Touch yourself under your dress. Do you like it? Now pull down the top, let me see. Now strip. Get on all fours."

Many days, many whores and then the decision not to do it. Not to lapse into that kind of life.

I'm lost, yes, but perhaps I don't have to be. Perhaps I can find my past, and maybe, I can find her. No more whores.

When the mail came addressed to Mr. Thomas Bradshaw, I knew that wasn't me. I ripped up the letters and then changed my name.

"Mr. Hunter? Mr. Hunter? Can you hear me?"

I came back, saw the doctor's face, saw his white beard and his round glasses.

"Yeah. Sorry, doc."

"I want you to go earlier. You've done very well, but let's see if we can't go earlier than those first months. Can you do that for me?"

"Sure."

I went way back. The accident. The car. The blood. The rank smell of gasoline. And a woman. A beautiful blonde whose skin glowed in the sun. A woman who made me smile like a boy on the last day of school. She wore little, but she didn't need to wear anything. When she smiled, I could only see the bottom of her face, never the eyes. But that smile, it was for me. Always for me.

"Oh, baby" I reached up for her.

"That's all we're going to do, son." The doctor's voice broke the spell.

Tears soaked my face.

"Mr. Hunter, you can put your shirt back on." Then came the

stenographer's final keystroke.

Walser's face hovered above me, his great paternal presence.

"Hey, buddy, we're gonna let you sleep for a little while, okay? The receptionist will keep an eye on you. Okay, we'll see you in a bit."

ךᵣᵣ-↓ך

"You there?"

"Yeah, Boss."

"Third?"

The image of a red neon sign with the word OPEN flashed in my eye.

"Conch, I know you're there, and we'll talk tonight, and Kairos is always there," I mumbled and walked out of the room into the foyer. Jeannie, the cute receptionist, was staring at me.

"You okay?"

"I'm fine—as long as we can—shut up."

She made a funny face. I waved a hand and said, "Inside joke."

Jessica Rollins-Gray sat dutifully behind her desk in Walser's office. She was looking particularly austere this afternoon, with her hair pinned back and her makeup done in a way that indicated she had taken no pleasure in its application.

I leaned on the counter and said, "I'm here to see Walser."

She didn't stop typing. She didn't look at me. She said, "Mr. Walser will be back in a couple of minutes. Would you like a cup of coffee?"

I let my head fall down into the crook of my arm. "Yes, ma'am."

"Then I will get it for you. Oops, I see you're too inebriated to stare at my ass today," she said, smirking as she walked past me. I lifted my eyes to her empty chair, a slight flush on my cheeks.

"I didn't know you knew," I said, because I had to say something.

"Knew what? That you slobber all over yourself every time I bend over to do filing?"

"Um…yeah. I'm sorry."

She returned to her desk, sat down as if she hadn't left and resumed typing.

"As well you should be," she said. "Your coffee will be ready in a few minutes. Cream is in the little refrigerator."

I looked at her. No hint of a smile. No emotion on that face. I was hoping for one of those It's Okay We're Still Friends winks, but I got nothing out of her. Just cold professionalism. That's what was so irritating about her. She was good. Too good. Perfect. And I knew she couldn't be. I knew that, underneath, she was just as scared and pathetic as the rest of us, only I couldn't prove it and the idea that maybe—just maybe—she wasn't, unnerved me more than the idea that she was covering it up.

I scraped myself off her reception area and mumbled something.

She paused. "Excuse me, Mr. Hunter, what did you just say?" She was actually looking at me now.

I turned to face her, halfway between her desk and the coffee pot, arms spread in some lame shrug of innocence. I felt like a drunk asking for a quarter.

"I said 'it's nice.' Your ass." I turned around and grabbed a cup. Her typing resumed. Somehow we were on even ground again.

When Walser returned, two others were with him: White and Rehnquist. I blinked, looking up from last month's issue of *Home and Garden*. My heart began beating in my throat.

Here we go again.

White was wearing a suit, which was too big for his lanky frame, and fancy, black shoes without any laces. He was smiling too much. His hair looked too good. His teeth were too white. His tie was loose like he'd been working too hard. A beat cop, turned dick, in a suit, and he didn't know how to even wear it.

Beside him, Rehnquist faded into the background, bald and spectacled, his round glasses the perfect size for his face. He'd never outshine White, and he didn't try to. He was wearing a suit, too, but he hadn't bothered with a tie. His suit fit him better, but he didn't look better in it. He looked outspoken, but I knew he wasn't.

I shook White's hand.

"Hunter! Goddamn it's been what, a year?"

"Nine months."

"Well," he said, "did you have a baby? Just kidding, man. Lighten up. I hope those nine months proved a sufficient furlough. We don't want burned out investigators."

"I'm not burnt out."

"Great." He turned to Walser. "Shall we?"

We began making passage into Walser's office as Rehnquist was saying, "Thomas, it's good to see you."

Inside, White stood near the corner, arms crossed, feet in a parade-rest stance. Rehnquist stood behind me, and Walser stood behind his desk. That put me in the middle of the room facing both White and Walser.

"Are we gonna sit down?"

"Hunter," said White, "I understand you underwent some treatment this morning."

"Is that what we're calling it?"

"I listened to the tape." It felt like his eyes were searching me, adding me up, probing for something.

I got this one, Boss. Let me get you ready for the ring.

Thanks, Animal, but if I get into the ring with White, we'll all go to jail and eat baked beans and watery oatmeal again.

"Yeah," I said.

He nodded and seemed to pick something out of his teeth with his tongue. "Be back tomorrow for another one?"

I thought about that for a second. "Why?"

"Because I think we can find something we can use. I didn't like the questions the doctor asked you. I have my own list I want him to ask. I think we can crack this one."

I looked down. It was getting warm, too warm in this room. I hated his manner. His imperial cop righteousness. I didn't want to placate him, but I didn't want to walk off this case either. It seemed the only thing they wanted me for was to probe my brain.

"No," I said, surprising myself a little.

"Excuse me?" He squinted with that cockeyed expression of disbelief. As if this were somehow tantamount to resisting arrest.

"No," I repeated, looking at him, not even feeling smug. "I don't think I'm gonna do that."

The moments that followed unnerved everyone in the room. White swung his head from Walser to Rehnquist in exaggerated disbelief.

"Wow, Hunter." He laughed insincerely. "Wow. Maybe you

should go back on furlough and get some more rest. Let me know when you're ready to play ball." Then he turned to Walser and said, "I don't know what you want to do with him, Doug. He's your boy. Maybe he needs to re-evaluate his priorities. What do you think, Rehnquist?"

Rehnquist shook his head. "It's up to you and Doug at this point. Hunter, are you unwilling to undergo a second treatment?"

Rehnquist just pissed me off. He'd spoken to my back, for one, but also he was hiding behind White's bravado and Walser's better judgment. But White was running the show, and everyone knew that if White didn't want me on the case, I wasn't going to be on it.

I didn't look at Rehnquist. "I want to investigate, not be investigated."

"Which is a great attitude," said White in an explosive round of renewed mock-enthusiasm. "And if we had any leads at all, I would clap you on the back and say 'go get 'em tiger.' I would. You know me, Hunter. You know I love to sink my teeth into a juicy case just as much as you do. But we got no way to go on this with the Vatican crawling up our ass making damn sure I don't touch one postmortem hair on those guys' heads. We can't decide whether to label these files under homicide, suicide or freak of nature.

"And, you know, I'm not gonna keep sticking my fingers into your head. I'm not. If we don't get anything on this round, I'll be the first to drop it, and you and me and Doug here can all roll up our sleeves and look elsewhere for clues. But, Hunter, we think you're our best link, and I've got to come up with something here before another one of these fuckers shows up or something else that's worse."

I felt he was sincere in that last bit. I knew he was, but I knew something else, too. They were looking at me as a shortcut, and that provided too much temptation. I knew that if I agreed to another round, nothing would come of it and another round would follow. Maybe not right away, maybe not even this case, but surely in the future. I had become extremely vulnerable up there, more vulnerable than I ever wanted to be again. I wasn't at all sure there hadn't been an effect created on me, because thoughts of Her were rambling around in my head, stronger now than they'd been before. I collected my thoughts. My words.

"I hear you," I said. "And I get it. I'm not going to do it again. Ever. Once was enough. I shouldn't have even done that."

White looked at his fancy shoes, hands on his hips. Walser looked down at his glassy desk top. I was letting them down, or so it seemed, though I wondered if I believed that. Then I thought of Dax and Ellen and Eva and my crazy crew inside my head, and I knew as solid as stone that these men in this room weren't my people.

This was not my game.

Finally, White threw up his arms. "Okay. We're done. Walser, over to you. Hunter, get some rest, you look tired." He walked past me. I turned to face White and Rehnquist as they exited. Before they closed the door behind them, White turned and looked at me. "One more thing. Hunter, next time address me as 'Sir.' It's just rude otherwise. Doug." He left.

Walser sat down in his chair. We looked at each other.

"Well!" he announced. "Coulda gone better."

Chapter 7

I didn't go home. I couldn't. I drove around then went to the park where I walked around and sulked. This was becoming habitual. Eva called me three times. I didn't answer. Then she texted me. I texted back and said I was busy and I would get back to her. I'd been blowing her off for days now.

I was despondent, crestfallen. I had wanted so badly to be on the case. When I'd left the office, Walser had said he would call me—that he would talk to White and see about getting me reinstated. I doubted it would happen. White was in charge of this thing and he despised me.

Bastards don't appreciate us for what we can do, man. They think they got it all wrapped up without us, Animal telepathized.

That's what doesn't make sense. They don't think that. They've said themselves, over and over again, that they don't have any leads. I don't get it. Wouldn't they at least let me stay on to investigate? Do my job? I thought back.

White's a pansy. You and me and Kairos and mother fucking Third can go take his ass. Fuck his shit up. Leave Conscience out of it. Just us guys.

Third's a girl, I thought.

Third's a nothing.

Whatever. We're not going to do that.

"As much as I might want to," I said.

I got in the Box. White had been adamant on how he wanted to use me in the investigation, and it obviously wasn't as an investigator. Walser was hoping to buy a little more time. He probably figured I could be persuaded to go for another round and at least gain another day or two to finesse White.

Why didn't this make sense? It didn't feel right. Too many holes. Why waste me as an investigator just because I'm not willing to go under and let some lab coat shrink my head? And did White really have cause to dislike me that much? That was possible, but not probable. He may have been a prick, but he knew talent. He would want me on that case. Specifically me.

Unless...

The thought occurred to me in the same moment that Third flashed the drawing. Dilbert at his desk. Only it wasn't Dilbert buried under a mountain of cartoon paperwork, it was me.

"Exactly," I shouted. "He's trying to keep me busy! He's afraid I know something he doesn't. Only I don't know it, either. So, it's a race between me finding out my past and him finding out my past!"

Sodium amytal would deliver the goods to both of us at once, which really meant he would have the information first, because I wouldn't be expecting ulterior motives. And if the happy juice didn't work, he'd cook up other things for me to do, things that didn't make a shit of difference on the case, but would sure keep me occupied. My hands would be full of things to make me think I was back on the team while sitting on the sidelines."

Oh, he was good. He'd almost had me. That whole scene in Walser's office had nearly made me feel guilty.

"Mother fucker!" I shouted. "Oh, I'm gonna fuck you and your mother! I'm gonna do exactly what you hate and go rogue and act like a goddamned, crazy cowboy!" I paused and turned off my phone. Then I removed the battery and tossed it out the window.

The starting point was obvious: me.

I had to find out what I was. No head doctor's hocus-pocus. I needed hard facts. I needed evidence that pointed to a logical outcome. So, first thing's first, I drove to the liquor store.

ᚦ ᛃ ᛁ᙭

By the time I pulled up to Dax's iron gate I was drunk. Not falling down drunk, just drunk. I had some recognition at that moment that I might be an alcoholic. When you can drive drunk and not act drunk, when you can do all kinds of things you would normally do sober, you have a problem. I had not been willing to admit that before, but I could now. Maybe because I felt I was on the verge of something big, something that would explain everything.

"Hey, Dax, it's Hunter. I need to call in that favor we talked about the other day. I'm ready." I was half afraid that Ellen wouldn't be there, that I had gone all that way for naught, but Dax's "sure thing" put me at ease.

I could already feel the dark delight creeping over me. The weedy drive grew ever darker as I approached the huge brownstone villa. The Wild Turkey was moving at a fine tune through me now. My crew was fast asleep. They weren't going to give me any reason to turn back. Perhaps this is what they mean by "liquid courage."

The dogs howled as I pulled up, but Dax was already standing at the doorway. His eyes gleamed in my headlights. He was wearing a pair of white, cotton pants and a sleeveless T-shirt that hung loosely over the contours of his muscled chest. He was decorated in malachite, lapis and moonstone. His black curls fell softly on his shoulders and over his forehead. He stepped into the pack of Dobermans and silenced them.

"You always drive drunk?" Somehow the angle of the light accentuated his subtle, but ever sharp incisors.

"How'd you know, Daxy?"

"I could smell you coming up," he said.

I shrugged. "No."

"You're back sooner than I expected."

"Yeah, I got a break in the case."

He furrowed his brow. "You found a lead?"

"Yes and no," I said. "Right now the lead is me."

"I got you. I'm just curious. The offer stands regardless of cases or leads. Ellen loves you, you know."

I swallowed. "Love is a strong word, Dax."

He smiled. "Well, not when we're talking about Ellen. She loves easily. And by that I don't mean she's easy."

"Is there any difference?"

"Yes," he said, "a lot."

"Once you take her, Hunter, once you drink from her, she will always be loyal to you, you understand? You have some responsibility after that."

"Loyal?"

"As loyal as any therian lover can be. You won't be her only one, far from it, but she will never turn her back on you, and you must never turn your back on her. Do you understand? Monogamy is not the issue. Loyalty is."

"I see," I said, glad for the monogamy clause. "Yeah, I can do that."

He nodded solemnly. "Very well." He turned and we went into the house.

Ellen was sitting in the main room on a comfortable collection of pillows. When I entered the room, she stood up at once and approached me. Her brown hair was done up in a French braid. She was wearing makeup and a white dress that wrapped around her hips. A band of the same fabric crisscrossed over her breasts. Around her neck she was wearing a red, lacey choker with a cameo of a black rose in the middle.

She was biting her lower lip nervously. We looked at one another in the muted candlelight. Her breathing was shallow. I could smell her sweet breath, the spicy perfume on her skin. She had gold bracelets on her wrists. She'd transformed from some kind of feral cat into a seductive woman.

"My God." I swallowed. "You're gorgeous."

Her mouth twitched into a smile. I tried not to, but thought of Eva. How could I do this to her? But then, she and I weren't together that way. Not anymore. And this was not that. This would not be a relationship in the common sense. This would strike a bond of another chord.

"I'm a little nerv—"

"Me too," she said quickly.

My head felt thick. I'd drunk too much. I hoped that wouldn't interfere with my performance. She moved close to me, her delicate hands encircling my waist. I inhaled and knew it wouldn't be a problem.

"Let's go upstairs," she said quietly. She took me by the hand, led me away from Dax's gazing eyes and the silk cushions. I wondered, in some quarter of my liquored brain, if Dax had any misgivings about this. Then I knew. He didn't. He had no reason, but generosity, to allow this interlude. And Ellen certainly was willing. No, this was the custom. This was the way in this…culture? Society? Maybe just this house.

She pulled me past the Minotaur and Theseus, in their never-ending death battle, and up the far marble staircase. I had never been this way.

Suddenly, I realized I had never visited Dax in this fashion, so familiarly. I had never sought his services as a therian. He helped me solve cases. He gave me information about legend and myth that somehow lived in the real world.

I pulled my hand from Ellen's.

"What's wrong, babe?"

"Oh, Jesus, don't call me that. I don't know what I'm doing," I breathed. "I think I'm going crazy."

She burst out laughing, and when I looked up at her, I started laughing too.

"You always think you're going crazy," she said. "Let's do this. I love you, whether you can accept that or not. I always have. Fine, I won't call you 'babe,' but not because I don't want to. Haven't you noticed my eyes on you since the first time we met two years ago?"

"You never said anything."

"Do you think I go around throwing myself at people? You weren't interested. You had other preoccupations, and I didn't feel like enduring rejection. You and Dax would go and talk for hours about folklore and fairytales, and when you'd leave, he would ask me what was wrong.

"At first, I was afraid to tell him, but after a while I realized he already knew. I told him how bad I wanted you every time you came over. Did he never tell you?

"No," I said. "He didn't—"

"Hunter, can we please go upstairs? It's dark, and I'm freezing."

The upstairs hallway, with its many doors, rambled crooked through the second floor. A ratty curtain at the end of the hall blew in a cool breeze. Using a skeleton key, Ellen opened the door nearest the window and pulled me in.

I was surprised. Despite the austere hall, the room was as cozy as a Hobbit hole. Beaten up hardwood gave way to oval, braided area rugs. A fire crackled under a marble mantel and bathed the room in a balmy, orange heat. The bed was huge and covered with a white comforter. There were tons of pillows, a coat rack, and other oddments from a bygone era. Opposite the bed sat the vanity, a big, oak affair that doubled as a writing desk. Its chair was layered with dresses, tights and lacy bras.

Necklaces lay in piles, along with slender rings of onyx, turquoise and picture jasper. Hair ties and powders and pencils for painting a pretty face and handheld mirrors and brushes and—no, not makeup brushes.

"Oh my God, Ellen, you're going to make me fall in love with you."

She blushed. "Hopefully you already have."

The walls held scores of them in varying sizes. All were set in Rococo style picture frames. Dax, the estate, the dogs, birds. It seemed nothing could escape her eye, but mine fell onto a nude self-portrait.

"You're—" I sighed. "You're amazing, Ell. I haven't seen art like this outside of a museum."

She steered me to the bed and pushed me down, then ran her lithe fingers across my cheek.

"I'm glad we decided to do this."

I was too, but reticent to say it. I felt bad about Eva and kept telling myself it had nothing to do with her, that this was research. Yeah, whatever. I stalled with small talk.

"Are you his only one?"

"Who Dax?" She plopped down beside me. "Not even. I've met two of the other ones. A man around forty and a woman about your age. There are others, I think, but I don't live here all the time so… But, this *is* my room."

"What's it like?"

"I don't know that there is all that much to say," she said. "I like being a vamp tramp. I like being here for him. He's very sweet, but then you already knew that. I don't know how his relationships are with the others. I don't know if he loves them like he loves me, you know, emotionally and physically. I know he has about a dozen of us and only the three of us who he really adores."

"Do you get weak, I mean, from blood loss?"

"Sometimes. But you know he doesn't need to drink me, right?"

"Uh…really?"

She shook her head. "Any blood will do and tonight you saw him drinking pig's blood, because he didn't want to spoil your coming. Human blood is best, of course, but pig is nutritious enough for his needs."

"So then why do you…?"

"I want to give myself to him. I don't know if you can appreciate the feeling of giving yourself over to another person so completely. That's why I do it. That's the high I get."

"You love him very much, don't you?"

"I do. I love him, and I love what he is. I love being a part of that. And Dax is so kind, so gentle. He would never even ask me to give to him. I offer it. Sometimes, Thomas, I make him do it, because I know he wants it."

"You ever want to become one?"

She stared for a bit, and I wondered if she'd heard me.

"He would never turn me. You don't know much about them do you?"

"Well, probably not."

She looked down. "They don't turn people like they do in the movies. Vampires hate other vampires or therians. They are beyond antisocial with each other."

I nodded. I knew that was true. I wondered when she would catch on that I was stalling.

"Would you let me drink from you without making love to you?"

"Is that what you want?"

"No, it's just a question."

"I won't make you, Thomas." She giggled. "And you don't even have to drink from me if you don't want to, and we can still make love. If you want. Either way or both or not at all, though I would be terribly disappointed if we didn't do anything. I want to make love to you, and I want you to drink from me, but I won't force you."

"You're very beautiful, you know that?"

"Thank you."

"You don't believe it."

"It's okay."

"When you're not here, what do you do?"

She shrugged. "I do my art. And I have a part time job serving booze to middle aged professionals. And if I'm not doing either of those things, I'm visiting my mom in the hospital."

She had a mom. Of course. Though to hear her say the word "mom" made me think of the word "pedophile."

"How old are you?"

"Now you're just stalling, mister. Come here!"

She planted long, lavish kisses on my lips, my neck. Her caresses inflicted a kind of hypnosis, and I became utterly possessed of her. I returned her kisses, feverishly. My hands found her hips, her small breasts under the fabric of her dress. We were heady from each other's touch and the passion that was building so rapidly between us. She shivered as she pulled away from me, as she unclasped the choker from around her neck.

Nothing could have been more erotic or more intimate. The two wounds previously hidden by it, bruised circles with ocher clots in their centers, were exposed. They presented the clearest reminder of how vulnerable she was making herself. I thought of Dax, stepping out of some foggy and forgotten London, seducing and feasting on this delicate Bohème. It made me want her ardently.

A soft moan escaped her when she put her neck to my lips.

The wounds leaked, and I was repulsed, but she pushed them at me and, in that action, demanded I do the next.

I did not want to do it, but her grip was firm and her intent was clear. I licked lightly and tried to ignore the salty flavor. I licked again and loosed the clot. Warm, coppery liquid bathed my tongue.

"Again," she whispered. "Do it again."

The clot broke, and involuntarily, I swallowed.

"Gentle," she whispered. "Don't suck, just lick."

Using the tip of my tongue to purloin small droplets, I drank her blood. Soon, the taste dulled, and it was simply the act. She held the back of my head, as if I were a babe suckling, and drew me down on top of her.

How much should I take in? I couldn't know the answer to that question.

"Make love to me, Hunter."

I withdrew from her, stringing a viscous line of crimson saliva and watching a trickle of slippery blood drip from the open wound. She had swooned so completely, eyes closed and a face so serene, that she hardly noticed I'd broken from our embrace.

I watched blood ooze. It stained her pillow, and my heart fluttered. That was all before I found myself gazing into the utter brilliance of a blue-white star against a black night sky. No, not sky, but space. The cosmos.

I'm dying...

You're already dead.

They pulsed, those stars. *Those stars?* It had been one, hadn't it? But I'd already moved closer, in an instant, and I could see them below me, those beautiful blue spheres, white hot at their centers.

A brilliant sun and its satellite, the latter infinitely smaller than the former. Were they moving? Pulsing?

What am I seeing?

Pulsing.

The one, true sun.

Pulsing.

Tell me what I'm seeing?

You're coming home.

Such clarity, such vision. Beauty beyond tolerance. Total freedom.

My God, what am I seeing? Third, are you catching this?

Coming home.

That time I got it. And rejected it. Hard. Because if it was true, I'd make it a lie.

You're coming home.

No! I screamed without a voice. *No, because I am not done yet!*

I fell. Down from the sky.

And just like that, I was back in the cozy room, gazing from a corner of the ceiling watching, below me, a burlesque porno.

Bed springs howled rhythmically while the headboard thudded away at the plaster. Two naked bodies engaged in what could pass for an Olympic sport in Transylvania.

Her eyes were open wide, fingers clawing, blood spilling everywhere.

I'm killing her!

Somehow I willed myself back in. Sensation swallowed me like Jonah's whale. I screamed, and then sucked in a breath like a man brought back to life. But still I wasn't in command.

Animal—more awake now than ever, even through the booze—was working the body like a virtuoso. I grasped for control.

"Ami, Elle est mienne! En moi, est la passion!"

"Animal?"

I had never known him to speak French. Christ, he barely spoke English. He was so strong.

Animal!

We were in the throes of it now, thrusting wildly, her legs locked around my waist. Panting, sweating, bleeding.

"Goddamn it, Animal!" Somehow I'd gained enough presence to shout, but nothing more. "I don't want to hurt her!"

Wasn't going to happen. Animal had the conch.

The body jerked, held and released. I could do nothing but enjoy. Orgasm rippled though me like atomic fission.

I dropped beside her in a pool of bloody sweat, my heart beating a stampede. Several moments passed before I had control again.

I reached for a towel and found a T-shirt. I brought it to her neck and held it over the wounds. Her breath came quick. Tears crowded my eyes.

"Elle?"

She burst into gales of laughter, and then giggled ferociously, arching her back, stretching her open wounds to leak blood frighteningly.

"God, Hunter! You. Are. So. Good!"

Chapter 8

"Hunter, stop it. What are you so freaked out about? Last night was wonderful! That miserable look on your face is going to make me cry."

"I'm sorry. It isn't you. It's just that I don't understand what happened."

"So, Hunter, you said a star and then you said, two stars, which was it?" Dax was lounging on his great pillows in a haze of incense smoke.

"Well, it was both. First there was one, but when I got closer they became two."

"Two of the same size or different?"

"Oh, different. Yeah, the one was huge and the other one was tiny by comparison, why?"

"And you say they pulsed?"

"Well, that's what it seemed like, though maybe it was just twinkling?"

"No," he said, "I don't think twinkling. I think you were looking at Sirius."

"Sirius, as in the—"

"Dog star. Or more aptly, the wolf star."

"If you guys are going to sit there and talk in code, can you at least teach me the key?"

"Sorry, Elle. It's the brightest star," I said.

"And thus the most prominent star in the constellation Canis Major, or the Big Dog," Dax added. "It's believed that mankind has had significant occult and psychic connections with Sirius down through the ages."

"So," I said, "you're certain I was looking at Sirius?" We had ruled out the idea of a Third vision and were all pretty certain that I had actually been out of my body.

"Well, yeah," he said. "You know, Sirius is actually two stars, right?"

Did I know that? If I did, I hadn't thought of it.

"I've always just thought of Sirius as the brightest star in the sky," I said.

"Yes, that is true, but it is actually composed of two stars, the other one is sometimes called the 'little dog,' or 'pup.' Anyway, that you say you saw two and they were pulsing, well, there's no doubt in my mind that you were being drawn toward the Sirius system."

"Okay," I said slowly, "so what does that mean?"

He took a breath. "Not sure. Did you perceive anything else? Any communication from it? Or sensations?"

I thought about that carefully.

"No."

"Nothing, huh?"

"Yep, nothing." I didn't want to tell him that I had kept getting the idea that I was "going home," mainly because I didn't want to admit that that had happened.

He shook his head. "Then I don't know, but I think it's pretty significant. Anyway, what was happening with Animal at the time?

"Making a woman out of me," Ellen said.

"And that's the other thing," I declared. "I have no idea how Animal got that good at doing that."

"What, sex?"

"Making love! Christ, he was like a frickin' French painter."

"Are you upset because he did it better than you?" Dax jested.

I exhaled smoke. "As if that's not bad enough, but no, it's that he knew exactly what to do with Ellen, specifically."

"So, when you came back to the body, you couldn't take it back?"

"No. I went to grab it, you know, from the inside, and I couldn't get a hold on it. I mean, normally when Animal has had control and I come back, it's just automatic. It's always just automatic with all of my crew. That's what freaks me out. This time he just had total control, kept me out until, well, it was done."

"How long before you got control again?"

"A minute, I guess. I was terrified that I had killed her. I mean all that blood and—"

"Far from it," said Ellen. "It was—Hunter, it was awesome."

Dax was lost in thought. "What does Animal say about it?"

"Nothing. He doesn't remember anything."

"He said something last night, didn't he?" Ellen asked. "I thought you two were talking."

"Yeah, he said…he said 'Elle is mine' and that the passion was inside of him. In French."

"That's fascinating," Dax said.

"What?"

"Animal speaking French and acting totally autonomous. How much blood did you drink?"

"I don't—

"About half," Ellen said.

I did a double take. "Half of what?"

"Half a pint."

"What? I thought it was like half an ounce."

She shook her head. "No, Hunter, you definitely drank."

I looked around the room like a confused math student. "Half a pint? I don't remember that at all."

Dax sat forward. "When did you pass out?"

"Uh, before we did anything. Like I said, I drank about an ounce, and then I was gone."

"That proves my point," he said.

"Which is what?"

He licked his lips. "Hunter, whatever else Animal may be, he is definitely therian."

"I thought we had already established that."

"I think he warned you against drinking blood because he knows. Well, think outside the box for a second. Where does Animal get his personality?"

I shrugged, but I knew the answer.

"Do you know?" asked Dax.

I sighed. "Me."

"Right. He's a version of you."

"That kind of makes me depressed."

"Don't be. We all have many aspects and those of us with the biggest personalities often have the most exaggerated alter egos. Anyway, under normal circumstances, Animal is, pardon this expression, filled with your blood."

"And?"

"And when you drank your ounce or whatever from Ellen, while it wasn't a lot, it appears to have been enough for Animal to have become possessed of *her* blood."

I thought about how much I was enamored of her in general. I really did feel myself yield to her.

"Maybe the combination of attraction and blood made for a total takeover," I guessed.

Dax shrugged. "One way to look at it, but yeah, that's my point. Animal took on Ellen's persona through the blood."

"Is that how it works in therianism?"

"In a way, yes. The blood teaches. In this case, it appears to have been more pronounced."

I thought about all this for a moment. "That would mean Animal could be anyone," I said. "Shit, with the right blood, Animal could become a parody of Howard Cosell or Oprah Winfrey."

Dax raised a brow. "It means, Hunter, that Animal can serve many masters."

That sent shivers down my spine.

I talked to myself as I drove back. Animal and the rest of the crew remained oddly silent, but I had become so accustomed to talking to them via myself that I carried on the tradition. This whole affair had been quite odd and, in many ways, frighteningly unnerving. I felt, for the first time, that Animal could be used against me. It was no minor thought.

And that bit about seeing the stars close up—my God. Not only did it make my stomach go queasy, but also it scared the holy hell out of me. That feeling of, well, of going home, was so eerily familiar that I just didn't want to think about it. At all.

I wasn't so sure about sleuthing down this path of self-discovery. Maybe I had lost my memory for a good, goddamned reason, and I had no more business going and digging it up than a grave robber has stealing corpses, aside from the medical research, of course.

When I got home, I showered, pulled the blinds and fell into bed.

I must have slept for twenty hours, because when I woke it was getting light out again. That little foray into the paranormal universe of therianism and occult star messages had really taken it out of me. I stretched and winced at the taste in my mouth. I kicked a leg out of bed and had just committed to the second one, when I heard: *where have you been, Boss?*

Oh, Animal my boy, what could you possibly mean?

I know you got piss drunk, but you disappeared. How'd you do that? Where'd you go?

That got my attention.

"Disappeared?" I said.

"Yeah, like gone, man. Like, I ain't seen you for two days or something."

"Did you see anyone?"

"Yeah."

"Who?"

"Someone else."

"Any idea who that someone else was?" I asked.

"Some chick."

I sat up. "You mean Ellen?"

Animal shrugged—meaning, I shrugged—and said, "I don't know. I never even seen her, but I felt her and she was a chick inside you. We changed down there?"

"No, Ani, don't worry." I got up and stumbled to the bathroom. From there I headed to the kitchen, hit the button on the automatic coffee maker and tried to find a clean cup.

"What are we gonna do now, Boss?"

Amazingly I had half and half that was still good.

"Um, work out."

I worked out like a berserker, not bothering to rest between sets. I started with my arms, then worked my pecks, abs, thighs and ended with six sets of burpees. Afterwards I felt alive again and hungry., It was a good hunger, which I sated on steak and eggs, two more cups of coffee and three glasses of water. Then, in post repast comfort, I dared to pull my phone out and actually look at it. It was my other phone, my track phone that no one but Eva knew about, and which is listed under the name Alfred Crackow, who lives in a PO Box.

"This is bad," I said fumbling for my cigarettes. Eva had called about twenty times. She was worried sick about me. Then I felt terrible about Ellen. Oh God. I had to let Eva know I was okay, but if I called she would want to talk for an hour, asking all kinds of sensitive and prying questions. I opted for the text message, but needed to send one that would not prompt a flood of responses, because I had to get down to the courthouse and do a whole mess of research.

```
<Ev, im fine. got a lot of
shit to pull down on this
case. This is a big one.
I'm buried like an ostrich
in research. don't worry
I still love you.>
```

It was true. The problem was me, not her. I felt funny about claiming such involvement in a case I had been kicked off of. She answered my text:

```
<I hate it but I understand.
I miss u. promise to call
me later when u come up
for air??>
```

```
<deal>
```

```
<;0)>
```

All right, I felt like an asshole. I wasn't going to tell her about Ellen. I just wasn't. I sped out of the warehouse and plunged into the downtown traffic. The sun was out, but I preferred fog. I got a coffee then made tracks down to the Hall of Records.

Now, I knew a few things about my past, technically speaking.

It's not that I didn't know anything. It's that I, myself, didn't remember it. For one, I knew I owned a property in Santa Rosa. I knew, because the family lawyer had told me so, that I'd had a brother named Edward, who'd apparently died around the same time I almost had. But I had never gotten the death certificate.

I'd gone through the family photos out in the Santa Rosa estate and found that he had been a merchant marine, a truck driver, a Franciscan monk and a jewelry designer. Not all at once.

In some photos he looked like me, in others I like him. It just meant we were brothers, not twins. The photos ended in 1999.

I had pawed though Dad's old business records. Bradshaw Enterprises. I'd found Mom's diary. She was a lush who'd remained married to Dad but did not live with him. She'd accepted a "quiet divorce," which wasn't a divorce at all, but rather a way to keep her happy.

I had seen my photo online, only to find it associated with two defunct social networking profiles, and also in some annual Policeman's Ball photo. I'd seen what I used to look like. The gut, the slouch, the expression of passive ambiguity. Not me. Never me.

"Yeah, hi, I need a death certificate for Edward Bradshaw," I told the Latina at the front desk. The heavily scented woman looked it up in her system and then looked at me. "I'm his brother," I said and produced a California Driver License that said "Thomas Hunter" on it. She didn't seem to notice.

She clicked around on her computer a bit, and I went to get some of the bad, complimentary coffee. When I returned she was still clicking around.

"I don't have a death certificate under that name."

"Huh?"

"Nothing at all," she said, blinking into her monitor.

"But he's dead," I said, wondering if that was true.

"In California?"

"Um…I thought so. But maybe not."

She shrugged defeat. "Nothing here."

I scratched my head and, just as she was losing interest, I said, "Can you do another one?"

She raised an eyebrow.

"Thomas Bradshaw," I said and then added, "My other brother."

She punched her keyboard, looked, blinked and said, "That will be eighteen dollars. Cash."

⊐7⊓?

I would have busted Walser's door down had it not been for Jessica Rollins-Gray. She pounced like a lean jungle cat and put my arms in some kind of sleeper hold. Animal was all jacked up, though, and I slipped out of it and shoved her off.

"Stop it!" hissed Walser. "Both of you! Jessica, stand fast. Hunter, sit down."

Jessica was breathing heavily, still posturing for a fight.

"He was aggressive coming in here," she said.

"And I thank you. You may return to the desk. Jessica, you may return to the desk. I repeat, Jessica, return to the desk." She finally did as ordered. "Hunter, in here, sit."

I didn't sit.

"When were you planning on telling me?" I blurted, holding out the death certificate.

Without looking at me, and as if nothing was amiss, he said, "Now, what's your blend of choice?"

"Is that what you do? Placate me with cups of coffee and bullshit when I come in here? Afraid I'll ask questions? Find out too goddamned much about what's going on?"

He paused and looked up like a professor deep in thought.

"And what is going on?"

"Waste him, Boss. Let's do this!"

"Shut up," I said staring at Walser, whose expression did not change. "You damn well know what I'm talking about. Do not play this game with me," I said.

He was pensive for a moment. He pursed his lips together then relaxed them. He smiled.

"Hunter. Thomas Hunter, I suggest we take a seat here, brew up some coffee and let the air settle, if you know what I mean. Jessica will go back to filing. The office will quiet down, and you and I will sip our coffees and discuss this as a matter of routine banality. Don't you agree?"

I understood his read-between-the-lines message. I sat. I still hated it, because I felt this was a tactic to get me to settle down. I felt like that in this office a lot. Settle down and get manipulated.

"Cream?"

I nodded. He left the office and closed the door. I heard him speaking to Jessica.

"You can drop the Richardson report on my desk. Yeah, I'll label it 'done' when I send it back to you."

It was his way of asserting the "business as usual" demeanor he wanted to portray, as if to say to his secretary, "You see, now, Hunter is sitting like a gentleman, nice and controlled. You're filing reports, and I'm musing over coffee beans. No paranormal, no intrigue, just plain old boring routine."

He returned and set down a steaming ceramic cup in front of me, then he sat down in his chair.

"I seem to be missing something," he said.

I pushed the death certificate across the table at him.

He took a sip and picked up the sheet as if it were the morning paper. He reclined, perused, and laid the document down. He sighed.

"The death certificate of Thomas Bradshaw," he said. "A good man and a good cop. What's the problem?"

"What are you?" I asked. "You and White, you just want to keep me quiet? Is that it? I thought I could trust you, Doug. Christ, I don't know who I can trust now."

He frowned in mock consternation. "I must be missing something here, forgive me if I am, but what does the death certificate of Thomas Bradshaw have to do with Thomas Hunter?"

"You're fucking with me. Plain and simple."

"Listen to me, Hunter. Very carefully. We both know—you and I— that on March twenty-sixth, 2007, Thomas Philip Bradshaw, the Second, died in a tragic car accident on Highway 1, presumably traveling to Santa Cruz, California. We both know that Thomas Philip Bradshaw was rushed to the Dominican Hospital ER, where he was pronounced Dead on Arrival. We know this. You and I.

"You, Thomas Hunter, are not Thomas Bradshaw. You, Thomas Hunter, go through a lot of trouble to make sure you are constantly reminded that you are just exactly who you say you are and no one else. Don't you?"

"I don't get it, Walser. What's your game?"

"Simply put," he said. "I like Thomas Hunter. Thomas Bradshaw died. Then Thomas Hunter showed up. Don't make it more complicated than that."

"How long was I dead?"

He only looked at me

"How long was I dead? Jesus, Walser, how long was it? Weeks? I was one of your fucking Incorruptibles, wasn't I?"

He held up two fingers. "Two hours," he said.

"Shit," I swore under my breath. Two hours dead? I would have been lying flat on a morgue table by then, while the death certificate was being written.

"Two hours before Thomas *Hunter* restored a heartbeat," he clarified.

I stared at him, incredulous. I wasn't even sure I believed him, but I knew he would not lie at a direct question like that.

"And that's when you claimed jurisdiction?"

He nodded. "More or less."

"And you left a death certificate in the system?"

He took a sip—slow, gentle and deliberate. "Thomas Bradshaw died, Hunter. Why not let it be recorded?"

I shook my head. "You know way more than you should. For the last time, what is your game? What angle are you playing?"

"I have no game or angle. I'm not playing some side. I like you, Hunter. I think you're a goddamned good investigator, when left to your own devices. And I think you suck when you're being smothered. I don't think you like to be fucked with. And certainly, with God as my witness, I don't think you're Thomas Bradshaw come back from the grave. I refuse to believe that theory."

"Then who am I?"

"You're you, Hunter."

"Damn it, Doug. You know, and you're not saying."

"I know you're Thomas Hunter. And I know you're not Thomas Bradshaw. Beyond that I don't have a clue, but I don't expect you to remember the Bradshaw family if that's what you're asking me. I'm not playing you, Hunter. You don't even look like Bradshaw. You ever seen a picture of him, or are you too scared?"

"I have, and fuck you."

"Then you know, too. He looked like a typical doughnut eating beat cop. That's not you, now, is it? You don't remember him? Oh, wow. I'm so surprised. Wanna know something, I don't remember the personal life of other dead men, either. So, why the fuck should you?

"Sharing bodies, passing bodies. What's a body, anyway? Blood, tissue, organs. A brain. You know better than anyone. What does any of that have to do with ghosts?

"Don't shake your head at me," he continued. "You know what I'm saying is the only thing that makes any sense."

It was true. "Then put me back on the case," I said. "Get White to put me back on this case."

He laughed. "I won't even try."

"Why?"

"Because the lone Apache hunts without leaving footprints. Because I like to keep it clean, and the cleanest way I know is to cut you loose. That's when you do your best work. So go out and do what you do best. Go hunting!"

Chapter 9

Back at the warehouse I brooded. My fingers were twitching so relentlessly that I finally went upstairs and opened the diary. I picked up the pen and let it go, Conch first, of course.

You're a complete jackass sometimes. How do you explain your immoral behavior with Ellen Stein?

How did you know about it?

I'm your conscience. You can't drink me away. Truly, I am interested in how you justify this action.

I don't.

Do you feel bad?

A little. But if I need to, to investigate therianism…

That is not the issue.

What's the issue then?

Infidelity to Eva.

I don't disagree with you.

So...

So in the real story, Pinocchio kills
the cricket.

דֶּרֶךְ

I called Eva. "Hey, you wanna get a drink?"
"Thomas! It's soap night. But I'm glad you called."
"Oh, shit! I knew I was forgetting something." I lit a cigarette.
"Come over and help me."
"Do you have food?"
"Um, let me see...rib-eye leftovers, a frozen pizza—the good
hand-made kind— hummus and...eggplant parmesan, does that
count?" she said.
"Be there in half an hour."
I showered then jetted up to the sixteen hundred block of
Haight Street. Somehow or other she had managed to acquire a
rent controlled apartment in the Haight that just happened to be a
storefront. She had mentioned something about her father and the
Hell's Angels, and then it got blurry. Suffice it to say, she had this
apartment for something like eight hundred dollars a month, and
when the tattoo guy below had moved out, she'd moved her shop,
The Craft: Witchery and Novelty, in. That had been four years ago.
She'd been making soap ever since.
Her light was on, and I knew she was up there churning the oil
and lye. I parked and let myself in. A blast of fragrance drenched
me.
"Whoa, smells good in here." I navigated through the tiny
hallways of the apartment. The amazing thing is that I actually fit
inside. San Francisco is known for these little monk cells it happily

calls apartments.

She stood over the kitchen counter, across from the Victorian nook where she and I had eaten chocolate banana pancakes on her birthday. The whole kitchen looked like a teenager's chemistry experiment. A beaker, labeled "LYE," sat off to one side amidst a dozen other small, metal bowls and phials, all of them filled with oils and crushed lavender, oats, sage. Then there were unlabeled ice cream tubs of what I knew to be coconut oil, and a big bottle of olive oil and, of course, a carafe of goat's milk—got to have goat's milk for satanic soap, you know.

I could smell the potpourri, and I could pick out the nuances of the different scents.

She flicked me a quick glance as she poured a brick mold full of soupy goop.

"Hey, Huntsy-poo."

"What do you need me to do?"

"You wanna make money soap?"

Not really. "Of course I want to make money soap." I went over and grabbed the ice cream scoop and started pulling up big balls of congealed coconut oil.

I mixed the rendered coconut oil with a pint or so of sweet almond oil, and a splash or two of patchouli and bergamot and then stood back to let Eva pour in the lye. She did it in such a casual manner, as if the stuff were sugar water and not acid that could eat through your skin. Once it settled, I operated the stick blender, which caused the chemical reaction known as soap, to take place.

She measured out cinnamon, dried bergamot and clover flower, and I dumped all that in and poured it into the mold. Ta da, money soap. Some money soap makers put an actual dollar bill into the mix. While this is a cute novelty in some circles, it does not sit well with real Wiccans, who are more interested in the mystic properties of substances like bergamot and clover. The combination made soap with a nice, silky lather plus all the right money-invoking ingredients. And as might be expected, it was her best seller next to love soap.

We did that for about an hour and a half. We made a lot of soap. All kinds. Swirly colors, black as pitch, oatmeal and other shit you could almost eat for breakfast. Right about when I'd had enough of the whole thing, she declared Soap Night to be at a close.

"Can I smoke in here?"

"If you must."

I leaned back against the countertop and waited for her to cover up the molds. The soaps would sit and cure for about a week before she put them on the shelves. They'd be ready by the time her present stock sold out.

Did I believe this soap worked? Hell no. But then I didn't have to. I will say this: her soaps smell and feel better than other soap. So, maybe that's all the magic you really need.

I was feeling acutely attracted to her at the moment. I knew I would, which was part of the liability of coming here. Last time we ended up doing it.

Boss, I think we ought to spend the night. I got a good feeling about this one.

This one? Do you even know her name?

Boss, I don't care.

Oh, God.

My fingers started twitching together.

"You seem better than last time I saw you," Eva said.

I chuckled. "Yeah, well it's the new case. I'm finally interested in something again."

"That's good. You hungry?"

"Oh, yeah, I was supposed to come over for the food."

She put the oven on preheat and then started making coffee.

"So, you're happier now?"

"I guess so," I said.

"What's this case you're on?"

"Um…bodies."

"That's descriptive."

"It's weird," I said.

"All your cases are weird. Isn't that your whole thing?"

"Yeah. You have any booze?"

"No. Have you been using your sources?"

"You mean, Dax?"

"Is he really a vampire?" she asked.

"Silver Rum is booze by the way." I reached for the Bacardi. "Yes, he is really a vampire. Though don't tell him that."

"Does he drink your blood when you go see him?"

"No, he has familiars for that."

"Familiars?"

As if conjured by the mention of his title, Charcoal jumped up onto the counter, slipped in some crushed lavender and declared his presence with a purr. She grabbed him.

"Well, 'lover' is probably a better word." I poured a glass of rum and downed half of it, then refilled.

"Like people offer themselves up to him to—"

"Yeah," I said. "He's a vampire. That's what they do. Anyway, I don't want to talk about Dax. Look, Eva the reason I came over tonight was because I wanted to, uh, talk to you about us—you and me."

"Thomas, you don't have to."

"Yes. I do." I held out my right hand and watched the forefinger and thumb jerk together. Staring at it I said, "I'm doing it so chill out."

I took a deep breath and gulped another swill of rum, which was taking the edge off Animal, at least his vocal abilities. Did nothing for the other part, of course.

The other part of Animal's heightened awareness expressed itself sexually. Being a man is bad enough, but at thirty-eight I had the sex drive of a fifteen year old. Eva just kept looking better the more I stood here in the soap den.

"Look. I feel like an asshole. I'm sorry. Eva, I love you. I mean you know this. Anyway, last time you came over and left, I just felt bad."

She shrugged. "I remember you being passed out on your bureau."

I thought about that. "Did I pass out?"

She shook her head. "Never mind. Anyway, are you seeing someone else?"

"No." I coughed.

"Okay. Anyway, I know all of this, Thomas, and I don't know what to say. We've had this conversation a hundred times and it always comes to the same painful stalemate. I don't like it any more than you do."

"Should I not see you anymore?"

She shrugged. "If you think it's best."

"I hate hurting you," I said.

"Is Conscience on your case?"

A spasm shot through my hand.

"I see," she sighed.

"Only because she should be. I feel bad, Ev. All the time—well, every time I think about it. It's like I'm just holding you—" I heard the tinkling of glass outside. The follow up noise left no room for doubt. It was the French-horn cop alarm: the Box!

ꓱ ♩ ꓶ⍺

I jerked into action and weaved through the labyrinthine apartment to the stairs. Outside, under the streetlight sat the Box, its alarm wailing. Glass littered the pavement on the driver's side.

"Goddamn it!"

As I walked up, I felt my hands, arms and upper body galvanizing; the muscle tonus was becoming taught, ready. Jagged edges of glass gaped up at me. I stopped and surveyed the area. I became aware of Eva standing at the door and motioned for her to stay inside.

On the seat lay a red brick with a note rubber banded to it. The whine of the alarm switched from French horn to rapid car-chase staccato and back again. I clicked the remote and hushed it. I grabbed the brick and removed the note. The message read: Boo!

Not a second later, I felt something coarse tighten around my neck. Shouts erupted in my head, then from my mouth, as if they'd struggled to come out. A "Not on my watch!" and "Kairos!" but, of course, Kairos was already on it.

Arcane sigils flashed through my mind as Kairos drew up a plan of attack. Then the plan took effect via Animal instinct.

I flicked my right leg back and connected my heel to my opponent's shin. I felt the thud and knew it had struck like iron. My rival slumped to the right, but retained his wiry arm hold. No matter, the next command code took effect. I doubted this one slightly, but went with it.

Left hand punch over right shoulder. This caught the attacker as he was collapsing. He was slightly taller than me, so my over-the-shoulder punch came up to meet his nose. It struck the philtrum, where the lip meets the base of the nose, a nerve plexus.

Good one, Kairos! I'll never doubt you again. A lie.

The punch had been short and stilted with most of the power escaping out the elbow, but the physiological changes that had hardened my flesh added impact.

He fell back, relinquishing his hold on me. I spun, knowing—or Kairos knowing—in advance the effect the punch had had. I kicked into a drape of black robes and struck the solar plexus. And then a funny thing happened. A thing I hadn't expected at all, because even though I was not using enough force to kill—not a man the size and girth of this assailant—he dropped. But more, he flopped to the ground as if all the life had suddenly just vanished out of him.

When the police came they tried taking my recorded statement, but I refused to give one. I explained what happened and gave them the brick and the note. They asked me who the victim was—*victim.*

"I don't know who the *attacker* was," I said, "and I don't believe I could have killed him with the force I was using."

The officer raised an eyebrow as if to say, "Yeah, jerk off, but you did kill him." I didn't know this young cop, fresh out of the Academy. I didn't know any of the officers who'd responded to the call. I hadn't moved the body, but I had gone through all six empty pockets of the black robes. The guy was naked underneath. He was so naked he was even bald. And one other distinguishing thing: he was wearing a neck brace. The kind people wear for whiplash. How the hell had he fought at all wearing that thing? He hadn't moved like a man with an injured neck. Or had he?

Anyway, other than his shaved head, he had two-day stubble. He was also wearing black boots, and to his robes was attached a cowl. It was no wonder I hadn't seen him. He looked like a shadow.

"This is my card," said the officer. It was inscribed with the name Detective Brian Figueroa. "We'll need you to come in and make a formal statement. Can I count on you to do that?"

"I'll think about it."

"Ah, Mr. Hunter, I have to inform you if you refuse to—"

"Maybe I'll have my lawyer make one instead."

He stopped talking to me. They dumped the dead guy into an ambulance and hauled him away.

I stood in the kitchen, staring into space and drinking coffee. Eva was cutting up the pizza. I had half a rib eye, potatoes and gravy. I could already feel the drag of having used up my internal resources. Kairos had pulled from other body systems, depleting stored nutrients to harden my fists and supercharge my kicks, which had left me really tired and very hungry.

"So bizarre," said Eva, quietly.

I shook my head. "Yeah. But not unbelievable. I've got to talk to Walser." I looked at her, finally, and gave in. "And I'm spending the night tonight."

Chapter 10

I left Eva around eleven in the morning, telling her to call me if she saw anything weird and then to call 911 and then to run away.

I got a coffee and cruised down Geary toward the Pacific Ocean to 21st Avenue, said hello to Mrs. Heidecker and went upstairs to my office.

I pushed open the door against an avalanche of bills, promo, fan mail and two boxes of Cuban cigars. What with my "busy schedule" it had been quite a while since I'd "gone to work."

I took all of it and piled it on my already over-piled desk. Then I began flipping through the bills without opening any. I threw out all the promo without looking at it and finally opted for a piece of fan mail. I knew it was *real* fan mail because the letter had been sealed with a very lipsticky kiss. Inside were a letter and some photos.

I looked at the photos.

Yeah, she was hot. And nude, except for a pair of thigh-high socks. The words "HAPPY HUNTING" were written in red lipstick across her midriff. Three photos, three poses. She had red hair.

Okay, well, I stuffed them back into the envelope, because I simply could not bring myself to toss them into the trash.

The slogan "Happy Hunting" had become popular amongst a small group of young women who had not sent me nude photos. They'd been cute photos, suggestive and sexy, but never nude. Until now.

I opened up all the mail from existing clients and sifted out the checks. The last one was from an old estate where, in order to find the Relic—which turned out to be bones, walled off a hundred years ago, a literal "skeleton in the closet"—I'd had to rent a cement saw.

Then I sat down and picked up a pen. My hand started to scrawl.

"Not now, I have to get messages." I had thirty-two of them. A new record. After trying to keep up with the first ten, I realized a good half were from the same person.

Avril Jensen had been calling daily, up to three times. Jeez, must be some ghost in her attic! But each message just calmly stated her name, her wish to talk and would I please call her back? Didn't sound like a prospective client at all and was too blasé to be a telemarketer.

It wasn't until message thirty that Avril Jensen said anything more.

"I need to speak to you about Edward Bradshaw. Please call."

Whoa.

I was stunned. Someone saying anything about Edward, the very mention of his name, was a big deal.

I picked up the office phone and put it down. I stood up. Paced. What could she want? Or know? It seemed odd that she should call only a few days after I had searched out his death certificate, as if that action had brought him back to life.

Or did she mean she was looking for Edward Bradshaw's ghost? That would actually make sense.

I went to her first message and checked the date. She'd left it before I'd gone for the death certificate, and she'd continued to call after I'd gotten kicked off the case.

The phone rang.

Okay. I hated being hounded.

After five rings I picked up the phone.

"Hi."

"Mr. Hunter?"

"Ms. Jensen."

"How did you know it was me?"

"Are you really asking me that?"

"I guess not. I'm sorry for calling so much. You're a very busy man."

"Yeah," I said, "I do a lot of other things besides sit by the phone."

"Mr. Hunter, I would very much appreciate if you would agree to see me tonight. Say, in an hour?"

"Give me one reason I should."

"Because I know how to find Edward Bradshaw."

I knew that whatever happened tonight and whoever this woman was, my life was going to change, permanently. You get those kinds of impressions sometimes.

Eva texted me.

Eva: `<you coming by tonite?>`

Me: `<sry. Its gonna b later.>`

Eva: `<like an hour. or more u think?>`

Me: `<more...everything okay?>`

Eva: `<you mean freaks in robes?>`

Me: `<yes>`

Eva: `<only one right now: me>`

Me: `<LOL>`

I dusted and otherwise tried to tidy up my awful mess of an office. Then I went outside to smoke a cigarette.

That's when she pulled up.

Chapter 11

She cut the engine. Metal creaked as it cooled. The door opened and a single, smooth leg swung out.

Time slowed, so that I wondered if Kronos hadn't rewired something in my ocular nerve. One leg became two, and then she was walking toward me. She was wearing high heels, a white skirt that stopped just above her knees and a skintight, V-neck blouse that didn't overwork the imagination. Her jacket fit snugly. Copper-toned skin was taught over sleek muscles. She was a platinum blonde. Red lipstick stained the filter of her cigarette.

Fuck.

Bossssss.

Don't act up. But be ready for anything. I don't trust her, but I might be in love. And that's a bad combination.

I can't take my eyes off her, Boss.

"Mr. Hunter."

"Ms. Jensen."

"Shall we go in? Or should we finish our cigarettes out here?" She was all business, which made me all gaga.

"Let's go in." I led the way up the stairs into the suite. Suddenly, my definition of the word "clean" begged redefinition. I was ashamed. The place was a dump: papers strewn all over, newspapers wadded in piles, layers of dust so thick you could grow a garden.

"I'm sorry," I said.

"For what?"

"It's not very tidy." I felt apologetic the way people are when they first show you the inside of their car. But it was because she came so well packaged.

She shrugged. "Yes, well it could use a woman's touch, I suppose. Don't you have a woman to touch things up?"

Was she hitting on me? Or was that just how she talked all the time? Truth: I didn't care. Now that we were inside together, I could smell her perfume. *Candy. A lot of friggin' candy.*

"Are we going to sit down or stand here staring at each other?"

"Uh, yeah. You can have a seat right here—let me move that. There you go."

She removed her blazer and sat with it folded across her lap. I took a seat across from her. Then I noticed my cigarette burning down to the filter. I squashed it out and handed her the ashtray.

"Thank you for seeing me," she said, tapping a tiny column of ash into the filthy, glass bowl.

I leaned back and tried to reestablish my composure. I didn't like being thrown off my game like this. I felt intimidated, and it had been a damn long time since that had happened.

"Yeah, well you didn't leave me with much choice."

"Why? What do you care about Edward Bradshaw for?"

"Well…he's my brother, for one."

She shrugged. "Is he? I thought your name was Hunter."

She knew way more than she was letting on. She was playing me. I stayed cool.

"You know my name was Bradshaw before—"

"The accident? Yes, I do."

"Well, you certainly know about me, don't you? I guess that gives you the upper hand, the old home field advantage."

"Except that we're sitting in your office, Mr. Hunter."

"Yeah, my office. Your terms. Feels better your way, I'm sure."

She smoked. God, I liked how she smoked. I wanted her to light another one just so I could watch her smoke.

"I don't mean to manipulate you, I'm sorry."

"Yeah, well you're doing a damn good job of it despite yourself." I had tried not to sound so scorned, but I resented the control she had.

I shook my head. "Look, I have a headache. I don't want to play games with you, okay? Let's just get down to business. You tell me what you know, and I'll tell you if I'm interested, deal?"

"Deal," she said almost sadly. She took a breath and licked her lips. A new cigarette was smoldering between her fingertips. "I knew Edward Bradshaw. I was his lover. He told me he was planning to go away for a while and, if he didn't come back after a certain amount of time, that I should go looking for him. He said he had a brother, Thomas Bradshaw, and that I should give his brother a key, and that his brother would be able to find the lock. Then he would find out where Edward went." She looked at me and took a drag, as if it were part of the sentence. When she exhaled she looked away.

"That's it?"

"That's it."

"You don't know anything else?"

"No. Eddy had a lot of secrets."

"And the key?"

"I have it."

"Can I see it?"

"Of course." She leaned down to get at her purse on the floor. Her left arm stretched, causing the sleeveless blouse to pull away at her shoulder. Something clicked audibly in my mind, some mental gear shaft slipping all to hell.

Oh shit! Boss!

I heard Animal shouting, I felt Kairos calculating the formulae, but they were far off, far and away in some misty, back alley of my soul.

Her position in the chair had revealed her bra strap and more of that rich copper skin, but something else too: a smudge of color in the shape of a fairy.

My breath escaped me. I clamped my fingers around her wrist and squeezed. The key dropped with a hollow clink. She winced in pain.

"Who are you?" The left side of her body slumped under my grip. Tears sprung to her eyes.

"You're hurting me," she whimpered.

"Who are you?" I squeezed her slender wrist, shaking with rage. "Tell me!"

"Please," she said breathlessly, writhing under my grip. "Stop. You're hurting me."

I released her and pushed her back. She crumpled in the chair, holding her arm.

"Who the *fuck* are you?"

She sniffled.

"Talk!" I shouted.

She wept and held her injured arm. "I'm sorry," she breathed. "Sorry for upsetting you. Please don't hurt me."

I stared at her in horror. This was no trick. The reality of who—what—she was struck me like a sack of cement. *She's the one, the link, the only one in the world that matters.*

"Oh my God," I whispered. "I hurt you. I'm sorry. I'm sorry." I went to her, dropped to my knees, took her into my arms. I inhaled the scent of her skin, her hair, her. I didn't care what her name was, or what our past relationship had been. She with me now, and that was all that mattered.

I breathed in the air around her as if it were pure oxygen. And then I kissed her. I kissed her over and over. I told her how sorry I was, again and again. I kissed her lips, her face. I kissed her neck.

"Stay with me," I begged her. "Please, stay with me."

Chapter 12

I woke just after dawn. The sun was threatening to break through the fog. The quiet of morning held my warehouse in a temporary stasis as fragile as a soap bubble. It felt as if we had existed outside the known universe. Outside of time. I appreciated those moment, as one appreciates the gently falling rain. But it was the uneasy peace before the storm.

She lay beside me. Beautiful. Sensual. She was turned away from me. The white bed sheet hung low, revealing her wonderfully sculpted back and that tattoo. I reached for her and as I did, a single ray of sun broke through the cloud bank and bathed the bed in yellow light. I'd seen this before. In my mind over and over. And now, I was living the moment, again.

Soap bubbles always pop.

She woke as I wrapped my arms around her. I kissed her lips. Our bodies touched. I pushed the sheets away. So quick was this passion between us. No time to wonder or doubt. It had been instant last night when I'd brought her home. We'd stripped naked before we'd reached the bed. Then twice, three times before sleep had divided us. Now again upon waking. Instant attraction. Instant need. I was kissing her wildly, tasting her skin, pushing her legs apart while she pulled me into her.

We made love. Vigorous, aggressive, border-line violent, as if some ravening hunger demanded obedience. I collapsed and rolled off her. We were breathing heavily.

"You're extremely good at that," she said. "I'm impressed."

"How often do you do it?" I asked.

"In the last six years, very little. Before that I was a prostitute."

"Oh?"

"But later," she said, sighing, "I worked as a private investigator."

"Interesting career move."

She shrugged. "Working as Girl Friday in a small firm got me clean. Not celibate, but clean of drugs and pimps and losers. Once I learned how to do background checks, I got really good at finding people."

"People get lost a lot do they?"

"They try. Especially if they've got something to hide. You fuck like a pro. Are you?"

"I've never charged, if that's what you're asking."

"But you've paid. I don't care. You'll never have to pay me. Even if I were still a working girl. I liked it too much, and that's payment enough."

I opened my mouth to speak, then heard a sound and shut it. She leveled a questioning glare at me as I brought my finger to my lips.

Oh goddamn it, no. No, no, no!

Footsteps traveled the apartment down below. Dishes clinked.

She shook her head inquisitively, tensing for defensive action. I waved it away, feeling a blow to my gut, like some bully had just knocked the wind out of me. Only I was the bully.

"It's—" I tried to explain, but I heard the telltale creak.

You get to know a house after a while. You get to know what the floors say when you walk on them, the one step with personality. The first stair to my bedroom is such a step. It always announces you. I pulled on a pair of jeans, then walked out to the landing before Eva could advance any further.

She looked at me, in that moment before the bubble popped, her eyes glad and hopeful, then confused. We didn't need to say anything. There's nothing you can say when your whole world falls apart. She titled her head and looked behind me.

Her mouth dropped open. The lines in her face deepened. Her eyebrows furrowed as she tried to form words with a mouth that would not speak them.

"Eva."

"No." She held up a palm. "Don't."

"Eva." I leaned over the rail.

"No!" she screamed, doubling over as if struck.

"Eva, please. It's not like that." I started down the stairs, but she ran. I caught up with her before she made it to the door and grabbed her. She spun around and slapped me. Hard.

"Don't talk to me! Ever again." Then she stood there, just looking at me, tears forming mascara tracks down her pretty face. Her lips held a terrible, painted-on smile. Terrible because so much sadness and hurt lay beneath it. I never wanted to see that smile again. Never wanted to hurt her again.

"You found her, Thomas. I'm so happy for you." She reached into her pocket and threw something against the wall. It clanged noisily. Her key.

Then she backed away as if from a wild animal, pushing tears from her muddy eyes. No words, just heartbreak.

"I hate you," she said, and her tears stopped.

"Evie…"

She picked up Charcoal by the scruff and walked out. I listened to the door slam. I listened to the car start. I listened to her drive away. I listened to the silence she left behind.

I returned to the couch and sat on the edge. Stared like the village idiot, confused and inept.

Avril crept down the steps cat-like in her sheet. She stood in front of me.

"Can I get you a drink?"

I nodded.

She let her sheet drop and walked naked to the minibar, where three bottles of Wild Turkey left the rest of the shelves bare.

"Bitch. We oughta wring her neck and show her who's boss!"

"Shut the fuck up, Animal."

Avril returned with two filled glasses and sat down next to me with her legs crossed.

"This ought to shut him up," she said, handing me a drink.

"You know about him?"

She looked at me without expression. "I've done my homework."

"What else do you know about me?"

"Are you going to hit me?"

"No."

"I know you're Thomas Bradshaw come back to life as Thomas Hunter. You have three distinct entities in your body. You think of them in your head, but only one is anywhere near your head, and even he goes through a psychosomatic audio channel to accomplish the trick."

"Animal?"

"Yes."

"Don't listen to her, Boss! She'll sell us out."

"Shh," I hissed and took another gulp.

She walked over to the bar again, and I couldn't help but admire. It was obvious that she worked out regularly. A lot of squats, I was sure. She came back and set the bottle down with a sharp, glassy pang.

"Shall I go on?"

"Yeah." I almost didn't care how or where she'd gotten her information, or if she was using me for some nefarious purpose. She was the link. The one I had been dreaming of, seeing, using the memory of. This was her, right here in the flesh.

She refilled her glass and topped mine off.

"Are we getting drunk?" I asked.

"If it helps."

"Continue." I took another swig.

"Animal is the one entity with vocal abilities, but only because he steals from you what he would say. He echoes your own thoughts and the baser portion of your personality. His life comes from your life. So, you letting him talk out loud is a clue to your—"

"I don't let him talk out loud—"

"Your intent. Now, the spacetime manifold, what you call Kairos-Kronos—I guess that's how it refers to itself—hardwires into your central nervous system and operates just below awareness to effect certain physiological changes and calibrations. Because this manifold operates largely below your basic run time awareness, you rely on Animal to interface directly even though Animal is only operating on a direct stimulus-response basis. So, Kairos sends a copy to Third to keep you informed. He doesn't—"

"Stop," I said. "Nobody could know all that. You've got a full, scientific diagnosis on me and—are you working with that shrink who put me under?"

She laughed. "Even if I knew about that, no." Then she looked at me and said, "Thomas, don't you remember me?"

"You already know I do. It's the how and where and when I'm oblivious too."

"I wasn't sure."

"I've been looking for you for years. It's driven me nuts. Where have you been? How do you know these things?"

I watched as the whites of her eyes went pink, yet she did not blink or look away.

"There's no easy answer to these questions. I still don't totally know what happened. I need to verify some things."

"Avril, you really need to tell me everything you know. We're way past the time for secrets."

She took a breath and reached for her cigarettes.

"Look, I like you. A lot. And I don't want to see you dead. That's why I am here at all, you understand, *at all.*

"Right now you're safe because you know nothing. The second I tell you anything about what's going on here, the second you take that key from me and start looking for the lock, you are in very serious danger. And me too. Do you understand what I'm saying? Your little identity crises—as long as you keep trying to remember—is the singular thread that connects you to a major criminal conspiracy, the likes of which you have no idea. You are standing on a nuclear landmine, and you think you're playing hopscotch. You're a child blundering with live wire. Do you get it? Tell me you get it."

"Yes. I get what you're saying."

"Good. So trust me. Can you do that?"

"I don't know. I'm trying to."

She put down her unlit cigarette. Then squared her shoulders and looked straight into my eyes.

"For whatever reason, know that I care about you. And have cared about you for a long time. Know that I come here under great threat to myself. I stayed away. My plan was to try and forget and let you forget, too. It almost worked. Then I got word that you were nosing around in this case. I decided to come keep you from killing yourself. You can be murdered, but it's more than that. You can be forever erased."

"There's a difference?"

"Fuck you. You hunt ghosts. You tell me, are they just echoes of some residual energy or are they trapped souls?"

"I don't know."

"Yes you do!"

"Fine."

"Fine what?"

"Fine, I think they're goddamned souls. Okay? Yes, I think they've trapped themselves in their dead universes, forevermore condemned to relive their past over and over again until God knows when."

"And isn't that why you do it? Isn't that why you go to these people's houses and do this song and dance of yours? Because, Lord knows, you're not in it for the money, right? Unless the Bradshaw Trust ran dry, which I highly doubt."

"Damn it! You know everything and you won't tell me anything! What am I supposed to do, beat it out of you?"

"You said you wouldn't hit me."

"Then what am I supposed to fucking do? You're doing it again. You're just pissing me off!"

"You're supposed to trust me! You were so quick to sweep me off my feet, bring me in here and screw me, but you don't trust me as far as you can throw me. What the hell kind of morality is that?

"If I would just lie to you and tell you I don't know a blessed thing, you would probably trust me implicitly. But no, I know all about you and you just can't stand it. You know I must be here to destroy you, just like your little girlfriend said."

"She's not my little girlfriend."

"Well she should be! Now, shut up and drink."

I took a deep breath and collapsed into my couch. "Oh my God. I am so fucked."

"Just wait," she said, "you won't believe how bad."

Chapter 13

Avril sipped a cup of coffee. I gave her my bathrobe, not because I minded seeing her naked, but because the fog had rolled in pretty good, and the ambient air temperature had dropped. I drank coffee too, but kept it spiked.

We'd made a truce since our last spat. It had consisted of two sentences:

Me: "I'll try not to freak out on you."

Her: "I'll try not to make you freak out."

I was playing with the key. It was attached to a small, metal tag with the number 211B on it.

"And how did you get this, again?"

"In the mail."

"A week ago, you said?"

"Yes, but with a postmark five years earlier."

"And there was no letter with it? Just a key in an envelope?

"Right."

"How do you know Edward sent it?"

She pulled a number ten envelope from her purse and tossed it on the coffee table. It was rumpled and looked old. The "return" and "sent from" addresses were identical: A. J., PO Box 77090, San Francisco, CA 94109.

"It's his handwriting," she said.

I picked up the envelope and studied it. I grabbed a pen and paper from the antique writing bureau and wrote the address out on a piece of paper. I compared the two and held both up to Avril.

"What's your point?" she asked.

"The handwriting is identical. Could have been anyone," I said.

She shrugged. "Proves nothing. Besides, he's your brother, you should have similar handwriting."

"Seems sketchy to me."

"So what? Post offices lose millions of pieces every year. This piece got lost. The envelope got damaged. When they found it, they sent it. Notice, he only sent one key," she said.

"And you've kept that PO Box this whole time?"

"Is there a problem with that?"

"No," I said casually, even though I was desperately trying to find one.

"Every safety deposit box has three keys. One for the bank manager, two for the renter. He sent me one. It means he has the other one."

"How the hell do you know that?"

"It's postmarked a day before he disappeared. He meant me to get it right away. Two keys. One in the envelope. It's an obvious way of saying 'where's the other one?' Meaning: 'if you find the other key, you find me.'"

I must have raised an eyebrow or something because she responded to it.

"He worked like that," she said.

"Okay. Whatever. We know it's a safety deposit box key because...?"

"Look at it."

I did. It had a long blade with square teeth. It almost looked skeletal, in a modern sort of way. I shrugged.

"So that means you've been living here in the city this whole time?"

"It's not my current address. A friend of mine received it. What's important is the key, not where I've been living."

"Fine. So, the box is in some bank in San Francisco?"

"I doubt it," she said.

"Where else could it be?"

"I haven't tried tracing it yet."

"How do you trace a safety deposit box from the key?"

"I don't know. But you're pretty smart and so am I," she said. "I bet we could figure it out if we tried."

"Then why haven't you tried yet?" I asked and quickly added, "Just out of curiosity."

She reached for a cigarette.

"I already told you. The minute we start looking for where that key goes, we're on the clock. Trust me on this one tiny, little thing. Once we start looking for him, people start looking for us. You may not know this, but you are very well monitored."

"Monitored or watched?'" I said.

"Monitored."

"Is there a difference?"

"In this case, yes. Watching makes it possible for you to find out. Monitoring is more subtle," she said.

"But you've come here; surely you wouldn't take that kind of risk unless—"

"I had to. You're not listening to me. Or not believing me. I already told you I took a huge risk coming here. And I already told you I accepted the risk because of you."

I inhaled. "The key is to a safety deposit box somewhere in... California, let's say. And we know this because of the little, dangly number thing, and the square teeth and the postmark. We know it's from Edward, because we know Edward is secretive and kind of cryptic and sending a key without a note is sort of his style, right?"

"More or less." She lit her cigarette. "Except for it being in California." She exhaled like some kind of female sex cat. "I don't believe for one second that the safe deposit box is here in the state."

"And why not?"

"Eddy was sly. Secretive, but not stupid. He was under attack. He needed to communicate in symbols and implications. It makes you want to look in San Francisco and waste your time.

"But he sent it to me. He knew I'd second guess everything, so he could afford to be enigmatic. He knew I'd rethink it over and over. He also knew he couldn't be too cryptic or random, or else I'd never get it. You understand? It's going to be obvious after we find out. It's going to be so Eddy."

"Cryptic and cute?"

"Enigmatic and sly."

"So, the next step is go to the locksmith?"

She rolled her eyes. "No wonder you're so confused."

"What?"

"What?" she mimicked. "How can you be so stupid, Hunter?

125

We go and dig in Eddy's background. We need more clues."

$$\triangle \ddot{\mathbb{T}} \times \mathbb{T}$$

We decided that we needed to lay low, which meant we needed to get out of the city. The old family estate up north was just the place to go.

As Avril and I took showers and packed, I noticed that Eva had left her bag in the kitchen. Not her purse, just a handbag. I wouldn't normally have gone through it, but because she wasn't—presumably—coming back anytime soon, I wanted to see if it held any valuables I should return to her. At first what I found didn't make any sense. Then I realized what it was: a letter, or more precisely, a conversation, carefully torn from my journal—the one Conch writes in when I actually sit down and let her demoralize me. It was written so frenetically I thought I'd been in a drunken stupor. Well, technically I had been, but here were two distinctly different handwriting styles. Neither of them mine.

Are you there? Ev............? HELLO...
HELLO...HEYYYYYYYYYY!

Hello?

Sorry. I had to get your attention. He's
so drunk he's passed out. He believes
his whiskey puts me to sleep. But I am
not like the others.

I didn't know.

As well you shouldn't have. Look,
I need your help. He won't listen to
me. He barely allows me to express

126

myself. I need you to promise me something.

Yes?

No matter what he does, you will help him do what he needs to do to find his past. Can you do that?

Of course.

You seem reticent, what are you not saying?

Well, I don't understand why you are bringing this up with me. I love him. Isn't it obvious that I will help him?

Eva, you need to understand something. Thomas Hunter does not know who or what he is. He is very confused. He is bound to get into a lot of trouble in the very near future.

Do you know who or what he is?

Even if I did, it wouldn't matter. He has to know. The members of his crew will kill him if he lets them. He does not know his limitations. I need you to be my eyes and ears, his—

Conscience?

Friend.

Ok

Promise?

Yes

Rip this paper out, he's waking up

I took the letter up to my diary and carefully went through it. I found the spot. The page had been so neatly removed no edges remained. I felt oddly violated.

"Fuck you, Conch," I whispered. "Oh, well." I knew it wasn't that way with Animal and Third and Kairos-Kronos. They were all subject to my command, drunk or not. That proved I had control.

Yet it unnerved me that Conch could be so invasive. I wondered if that was what Avril had meant when she'd said I was being monitored. I glanced over toward the bathroom, where she was showering. Then something she'd said occurred to me. Earlier, after Eva had left and Avril had been psychoanalyzing me, she had referred to "three distinctive entities."

Three.

But Conch made four.

Could Avril really *not* know about Conch? And for that matter, what exactly was Conch?

I heard Avril step out of the bathroom. She put on the same outfit she'd been wearing the previous night.

"You're going to need more clothes, aren't you?" I asked.

"We can stop once we get out of town."

"Do you think we'll be followed?"

"We'll take my car. It's a rental."

I wondered how I had missed that. Of course, I hadn't been paying attention to her vehicle.

"Plus," she added, "we'll make sure we're not tailed."

I was glad that I'd had her park in the garage. After the brick, I didn't want any more broken windows. Going to the estate up north would put some distance between ourselves and shaved-headed Satanists.

"So, maybe I should ride out in the back seat under a blanket with you driving, until we get out of town?"

She nodded. "Good idea."

"Yay! One for me."

She didn't respond.

I shoved all the whiskey bottles into my duffle bag and zipped it up.

"Let's go."

We rode out, with me under a coarse wool blanket in the backseat and her driving all cold and business-like. She looked a thin version of Marilyn Monroe, in her sunglasses and cherry red lipstick, which somehow added to the whole romance of the thing. Who was I? Humphrey Bogart playing Philip Marlowe? More like Inspector Clouseau.

She passed through the tollbooth, and I heard the tires drive over the Golden Gate Bridge. Then she said, "You can come out now."

I popped up. "You even talk like one."

"What?"

"A movie star PI." I was only latently aware of how nerdy I sounded.

This time she did smile. Then she reached for a cigarette. I sat back and enjoyed being chauffeured. I missed the Box, however, and knew I would continue to miss it until I was back in the cockpit. I felt like I shouldn't be cutting it out of an adventure. That car had been there through thick and thin.

"You know how to get there, right?"

She looked at me through the rearview. "I know how to get to a boutique for new clothes. After that you can drive."

Oddly, she got off the freeway in Sausalito and drove past the little café where I had ogled the horse society women. We parked and went shopping, but it wasn't the kind of shopping I'd expected. Avril went into three stores and bought clothes off the rack, without even trying them on. In each boutique, she entered, did not return a greeting, pointed to what she wanted and had the girl on duty pull out all size twos. She then paid with a wad of cash that never seemed to diminish. We finished inside of half an hour.

"You amaze me," I said.

"What now?"

"I have never known anyone like you."

"What's your problem?"

"The way you bought your clothes. How do you know they are even going to fit?"

She smiled thin-lipped. "I know my size. I know what looks good on me. Besides, if they don't fit, I can just go naked, right?"

We arrived in Marshall, California a couple of hours later, picked up groceries and firewood and headed to the estate, which was situated near the not so famous Tomales Bay.

The house—well, mansion—stood about as far away from civilization as one could get and still remain on land. Standing guard over the grounds were enormous, sprawling live oaks. Great, big, mossy-backed things, drooping their noble branches nearly to the ground.

We wound our way through an overgrown road to the house, an old French provincial with deep, brown brick-work, steeply pitched roofs and arched windows. The thing was beautiful, even while it was in a shambles.

I'd been out here a handful of times in the last five years. I'd even purged it of ghosts, of which I had found two. In life, they had been mother and daughter. Any normal person wouldn't have noticed them.

I'd had a security company update the alarm system and make weekly rounds, just to alert me if anything got really off. It never did.

I opened the door and made a beeline to the alarm console, where I punched in the code. It beeped and disarmed. The house smelled musty. Avril walked in and looked around. To my surprise, she said, "Cute."

I plugged in the refrigerator so we could put the groceries away, and then I pulled dust-ridden cover sheets off the furniture. Décor and appointments were somewhat spartan. I'd thrown a lot of stuff out or given it to antique shops, and then never replaced it. Some things remained, however, like the leather couches in the main room and a host of posh, Victorian, antique chairs that had been reupholstered. Oh, the place had three four-poster beds and all kinds of cherrywood desks and chests and stuff.

"Do we have internet?"

I shook my head. "The phone guy's gonna come out."

"How long will that take?"

"They're scheduled for tomorrow," I said. "While you were showering, I was working."

She softened, then smiled. "That means we have all kinds of time to kill." It was the way she said 'kill.'

We went upstairs to the cloistered master suite, with its slanted ceilings and other nook-like accoutrements, and put fresh sheets on the bed. Then she said, "Come here, I need a fix."

Chapter 14

I rummaged for what I could find having to do with Edward: a handful of blurry photos and a partially written journal.

"How well did you know this guy?" I asked.

"Not well enough," she said.

I'd already found the photos on a previous visit, but the journal was new. Its pages hosted a variety of archaic, hand-drawn diagrams and pentagrams, but more: scores of sigils.

They were so numerous and so painstakingly intricate that they made my head swim. It looked like the work of a bored speed addict. Many of them had weird titles, such as Roubriaộ, Ischure, Ma, Döö and others.

After scanning through it, one thing stuck out. Something he'd written in the second to the last entry.

> *There are two ways to die. Out the top*
> *and out the bottom. One could argue*
> *that the first is not death. But I'm not*
> *arguing. Even death is relative.*

It was the opposite of what I would expect from someone who'd written about pentagrams and spells. From what I'd seen in my dealings and travels, people who were into that kind of thing romanticized death. They made it out to be this wonderfully macabre affair, where corpses dressed in cravats and ascots and spoke eloquently while musing over lost love. Here was a very clinical approach.

The last line read:

> *Some might think it anti-religious to*
> *attempt to cheat death, but I am not a*

religious person.

I put the book down and turned to the task of finding the lock. I got online and started searching safety deposit boxes. After a few dozen searches, I had narrowed it down.

"Looks like a Mosler Diebold," I called out, showing off.

Avril looked at me over her laptop. "Excuse me?"

"The key looks like a Mosler—"

"A nineteen-twenties box door, three-point lock, fifty-six hundred series, yes I know."

"Aaaallll right. So! Since you're light years ahead of me—wait, I thought you hadn't done a trace on the key yet?"

She shrugged. "I thought it was obvious."

I leaned back in my chair and stared at the ceiling.

"What you can do to help is tell me where Edward was born," she said.

"California."

"Is that where you were born or where he was born?"

"Both of us." Actually, I had no idea.

"Did you ever pull his birth certificate?"

I shook my head, suddenly confused. "Why would I—"

"He's your brother! And you've supposedly been searching high and low for your past, that's why. My God, Thomas, it's no wonder you haven't found anything. You're not even looking."

That stung. She was two different people. One in bed, another on the street.

Careful, Boss, this bitch is gettin' uppity.

"I've looked."

"You haven't. From what I can see, you're playing a game with your amnesia."

"What's that supposed to mean?"

It means put her in her place and get her cookin' and cleanin'!

I had almost forgot Animal was there. The minute she'd started talking about my past, he'd come to the party.

Shut up!

"You're making a game of forgetting your whole life. Just one big confused and forgetful episode. Romantic, perhaps, but not very practical."

She wasn't just hitting a nerve. She was shoving a nail into my cerebral cortex. Animal started to howl.

"Animal, please," I said, "or I'm just going to drink you away."

She laughed. "He just can't stand it, can he?"

"What?"

"Hearing this. It's true, though. You should already know everything about your brother, your father and your mother. That you don't just proves what I'm saying. Your forgetfulness is just an excuse to be reckless and irresponsible. You need to stop acting helpless and making a meal out of all this 'forgotten past' stuff. You could have figured it out by now, if only just by piecing it together through public records. Five years is more than enough time to do that. And with plenty of slack-off time to boot."

Conch had nothing on this chick.

"Apparently, you had to come rescue me," I said.

"Once the key came, I could have left you to die. All I'm saying is you should know more than you do. If you were really trying."

I held up a hand. She'd just exhausted me. She'd thrust where I'd expected a parry. She'd gone for the heart where I'd expected a flesh wound.

"You're right. Maybe I don't want to know. I don't want to argue," I said.

"I need to know where Eddy was born. I'm trying to figure out which banks are using old-style Mosler boxes, but it's impossible to search nationwide for something like that. Eddy wouldn't send me a key with no other information unless he knew I could figure it out. I'm going to start in Seattle, because he loved that city, but after that I'm stumped."

Then it hit me. Like unexpected flying dog shit in a paper bag. I had no idea what I'd been thinking these past days. I'd been shanghaied. Lock, stock and cock. My mind had been hijacked through my penis.

"Damn me."

"What?" she said scornfully. *Scornfully*. She hated me. She was one of those weird, crazy, hot chicks who hated the men she slept with. She was just using me to go pop the safety deposit box so she could run off with the loot. She used sex like a drug so I wouldn't ask any questions.

"What, Thomas?"

I was glaring at her. "I'll go look for more clues on Edward," I said, getting up. I had to go somewhere else. I had to figure out what to do. Leave. Take the car and leave her here and—but there was a part of me that believed her.

I crept up two flights of creaky steps to the attic rooms, where old cardboard boxes had been stacked away. I'd gone through most of them. She was right, too, which I hated. I was milking my amnesia.

But why?

The room up there was long and narrow, like a hallway, with half-ceilings slanted parallel to the pitch of the roof. A huge, king-size bed took up most of the far end, where the room widened. Along the slanted ceiling-walls was a series of short, square cabinet doors, behind which lay a deep trench of storage space. You couldn't stand up inside, since the space tapered off to the triangle edge of the roof truss, but a lot of stuff could be shoved in there.

One of the things I had done here was patch this side of the roof. So the water damage should have ceased, but the mold had already done some good damage to the stored goods.

I leaned back against the bed and picked up a handful of photos and papers.

Avril is the link between what I am and what I was. That's her significance and why I have been so enamored with her. It's what she represents, not what she is.

I laughed out loud.

That I found her so ridiculously attractive was a bonus—or hook, but for God's sake, I could not forget what I was doing. And I couldn't argue that making love to her made my head quiet, and with no drugs or booze, either. That had to be a good thing, right?

I pulled a moldy photo out of the pile, a baby picture that was labeled "1971" in faded ballpoint. In the same pile a birth certificate copy: mine. Prime baby keepsake stuff. I dug deeper and found a letter on "Office of the Mayor" letterhead.

"As you know, this situation requires urgent and effective action…blah, blah, blah…and…holy shit…Pursuant to my authority, Captain Thomas Bradshaw is hereby and forthwith awarded the appointment of Chief of Police? Are you fricking kidding me?"

I read it three more times. No wonder all those beat cops stared at me now.

"Walser, you liar! Of course White hates me!" How could I not know this? I checked the date. A few days before my accident. Chief of Police for a day.

I didn't find anything more in the box, other than rotting baby photos, three bibs and a spoon. So, I crawled back into the attic storage, pulled out another one—complete with a family of spiders and a dead centipede—and dug through it. I didn't see a birth certificate, but I found something just as good: a social security card. Edward's.

When I got downstairs, Avril was on the phone with a bank asking about make and model of safety deposit boxes. Upon seeing me she begged off.

She took the card. "Perfect."

I came around behind her chair and watched her google the first three digits of the social security number: 384. That meant Michigan.

She stood up. "Make a list of every bank in Michigan. I'm going to find out if there is any way to see what county or city this came from."

I produced a list of banks in Michigan. There was one huge, long page with hundreds of branches divided up amongst them.

"There's a lot of them," I said. "Oh, hey I almost forgot, I found this—"

"Start calling. Ask if they have safety deposit boxes or which branches have them."

"Look at this." I pulled out the letter.

"Does it have anything to do with what we're doing?"

I shrugged. "Probably not. Just an old accolade from a bygone era."

"Then show me later. We need to work on this case right now."

I sighed. Then I picked up the phone and clicked on the first name on the computer list. That's when it dawned on me.

"He was clever right?"

"Yes. Very."

"But not so obscure you couldn't figure it out if you tried and knew where to look, right?"

"Yes," she said. "Start dialing. We don't have forever."

"It's probably this one. The Huntingt—"

"There is just no way to narrow it down further using the SS number. What did you say?"

"Huntington Bank. *Hunting*…ton for the *box*. *Hunting*ton for the…*past*."

She was already behind me, staring at the computer, her breasts resting on my shoulder.

"And it has more branches than any other bank in the area, which puts it first on the list," she said.

"Hidden in plain sight," I observed.

"That's my Eddy."

She took the mouse and found a number for the bank then dialed it on my phone.

"Give me all the Detroit area ones," she said into the phone. She scribbled down thirteen branches and wrote *SD boxes* above them. She hung up the phone. "Book two flights out of Santa Rosa for Detroit ASAP. I'm going to shower and pack up."

"Whoa," I said. "Just like that, we're tearing off to Detroit?"

"Yep." She was already stepping out of her underwear. "Find out which branches in Detroit have safety deposit boxes."

דוּיִ֗דּ

The first flight out was at five thirty the next morning. The rest of the day we poked around online to find more about safety deposit boxes and banks and where to look should we strike out on Huntington. Then we went to bed and made love. Really, though, you couldn't call it "making love."

When we touched, somehow all the squabbling and cold shoulders melted into meaningless quibble. And we couldn't just do it once and have a cigarette. It was three or four times and half a pack of cigarettes. Then we lay there drinking coffee and talking.

"Tell me about you and this Eddie," I said.

"I loved him," she said. "I really loved him. But so many other things were happening. We were in such danger together. Maybe that's what brought us so close so fast."

"We're in danger together," I said, "right?"

"Yes, and look how close we are."

We did it again and went to sleep.

Flying dreams always amaze me. The effortless gliding up through the quiet dark house into the sky, or the ones where you just sort of go from rooftop to tree to telephone pole. I love them all. I usually just let myself go. I am continually awed by how clearly you can see the environment in these dreams.

As I floated through the estate, everything was just as it had been during the day. Even down to the dirty dishes in the sink. I figured I would float out of the house and above it, but in this case, I began gliding into a dark corner, the V of two bookshelves. My body, face first, pressed up against the books. I could smell the dust and the old paper. I don't know how long I hung there, but as I did, my body pushed forward more and more firmly, until it became uncomfortable.

This flying dream sucks.

Then the bookshelves parted and sent me into a terrifying freefall.

If I'd still thought I was dreaming, I was having my doubts. Just as I expected to break my legs, the fall caught, and I slid down light as a feather.

Practically pissing myself, spine tingling like a teenage girl's, I drifted down into the contours of a hidden room with phosphorescent lights.

In the center of the room lay the circle, glowing and pulsing with energy. I only half realized that Third was turned on, though I had not made a request. I moved closer to the circle, seemingly by thought, like the night with Ellen when I had moved so effortlessly toward the Sirius system.

The circle spread out below me, a radiant kaleidoscope of intersecting lines and symbols. Pentagrams within pentagrams, layered as intricate as any MC Escher wood carving.

I struggled to make sense of the arcane symbology.

I slipped toward the circle, entranced and enchanted with the promise of what secrets could be divined there. Knowledge, power, answers to the deep mysteries of the universe. And myself.

My feet settled down onto fine grain sand before an altar, where a glossy, black plate shone dark and dazzling.

I stared into it, lost myself in its polished midnight hue, and reached out to touch it. That's when I saw a familiar image move inside the glass: a shadowy tail, serrated and prehistoric. Before I realized what was happening, something bit into my chest.

ך ּ צ אׁ

"Thomas! Oh, God!" Avril was snapping her fingers. "Thomas? Thomas!" Then I felt a hot sting on my cheek.

"Hi."

"Thank God! Come here."

She wrapped her arms around me. The lights were impossibly bright now. We both went down to the floor. I was shivering in a cold sweat.

"Wh-wha-what happened?" I shivered. My teeth were chattering like a windup toy, and my chest was aching.

"I don't know," she said. "You were sleepwalking. I heard you."

"H-h-heard me?"

"You were screaming." She held me, rubbing warmth back into my arms.

"I was?" I remembered what I had seen in the disk. "Oh, right. That demon thing, again."

"Demon thing?"

"Yeah. I never told you. There's a...there's a thing that's following me. It's a—"

"We need to get out of here," she said, sternly. "We need to get to Detroit and solve this case, fast, or there's going to be a lot more demon things than that."

"You said I was on the clock once we started looking," I said. "But I think I've been on the clock since like a week ago."

"Proves my point all the more," she said. "Come on, I'll help you."

I was stiff getting up and pain was racketing through my upper body. I wobbled on my feet.

"Hey, you okay, Thomas?"

"Wait," I said coughing, clutching my chest as the pain slowly drained away. "What is this place?"

The room looked different in the light, its spook-factor faded quickly. We were standing outside the circle. I was staring at the pentacle and all the symbols it held.

The characters appeared to be Latinized, as if I might be able to read them, but closer inspection proved otherwise: backwards Ls, inverted crosses and strange Arabian looking symbols.

"Thomas, come on."

"I've seen this before! This is what Kairos uses to do the calculations. He's always flashing them to me on little cards and—"

"Thomas, please!"

Boss, I don't like this shit.

"Thomas, we have to go. We can't miss the flight. Please. It will still be here when we come back."

"These cards have more of the—"

"Thomas, please!"

"These are the cards Kairos uses!" I said. "There are so many answers right here in this place."

"No," she said. "This is not answers, Thomas. This is black magick."

On the altar a towel was draped where the black plate had been. I reached for it.

Avril caught my wrist. Her eyes were boring into me now. "Drop it. We are going. You and me, right fucking now."

< ~ᛒᚲ

Next stop: Hamtramck, Michigan, the old Merchants and Mechanics Bank building, now the Huntington Bank building, where they have old 1920s Mosler safety deposit boxes.

Chapter 15

Hamtramck was cleaner than the rest of the metro area and a trifle more upscale. Truth, I wasn't really paying attention. I was anxious about finding a match to the key and seeing what lay inside this mysterious box.

We parked on Holbrook and walked around the corner to the bank. Nice place, vaulted ceilings, some kind of Gothic revival architecture. My kind of place. I approached the pretty black girl, who asked if she could help me, and showed her my key. One look in her computer produced a rigid head nod and a direct call to the manager. A couple of moments later an older gentleman in a well-fitting navy blue suit appeared.

"Mr. Bradshaw, how are we today? Been some time, hasn't it?" the bank manger pumped my hand like a politician.

"Yeah, I suppose it has," I said.

"What can we do for you today, sir?"

"Well, Jeeves, I was thinking I would like to close out my safety deposit box." I waited, expecting some kind of resistance.

"Oh, but of course," he said. "Right this way."

What fascinated me was that this man, this bank manager from a city I'd never been to, recognized me to the point of not even asking for ID, and it had been several years since he thought he'd last seen me.

We went to a special area behind maglock doors, where he escorted me to the ever more secret vaults, his demeanor so friendly that it bordered on snively supplication. I felt like a young Daddy Warbucks come to take possession of his million-dollar diamond necklace. We walked down a line of old, sturdy looking Mosler boxes with their round, brass keyholes and bright steel doors.

The procedure for opening the box was something of a formal ritual. The manager had his guard key. With a practiced flourish of historical etiquette, he inserted it into the top lock. Then he moved aside and gestured for me to insert mine. He stepped back, somehow melting into the shadows, to allow me to examine or remove contents at will. It didn't take long. I pocketed the item and returned to the front, feeling decidedly cheated.

I signed another paper to close out the box, and then to my surprise, the banker expressed his assumption that I would be leaving my account open.

"Well, uh—what's the balance now?"

"Let me check, sir." He nudged the pretty black girl aside as though she were a piece of furniture and typed at lightning speed. "Yes, just under ten million at nine million, nine hundred and eighty thousand, seven hundred sixty-two dollars and ten cents, sir."

I nodded slowly and tried not to blink too much.

"Yeah." I said. "I'm gonna wait on that. I'll let you know."

"Very well, sir. Is there anything else I can help you with today?"

"No, that's pretty good what you did."

"Have a good day, won't you?"

Outside Avril turned to me. "What is it?"

"It's—"

Boss, ten o'clock!

And once again, I didn't have a chance to complete my sentence. "Duck!" I said.

She dropped as I swung and connected with a mustached man in tight-fitting painter's garb. The crack was audible. His head went sideways and then down, where he paused, as if I'd knocked a tooth loose and he was feeling the empty socket with his tongue. When he brought his head up level again—no hurry at all—he was smiling. Then his fist shot straight out like a mechanical boxing arm and pummeled me.

"We need more armor!" Wasn't sure who'd said that, but I was up and back at it with a Kairos-organized arm-path-trajectory punch. It struck like an apple hitting a brick wall and split Mustache Man's lip, which opened a small geyser of pinkish lymph.

That's not blood!

I didn't have time to analyze it. He was leaping and reaching out with both arms, rapidly closing the space between us. Two enormous hands clapped my ears, and I dropped to my knees, my head thrumming like a bell clapper.

"God, that hurts!" my mouth screamed.

Kairos!

But it was Kronos who answered, with a flood of opiate endorphins. I stood up and shook it off.

Animal-Kairos galvanized my foot, and I kicked and struck Mustache Man's groin. Moustache Man dropped, but didn't make a sound. His head shook like a dashboard trinket, and I knew I'd bought time. Over his coveralls, he was wearing two wrist splints and a back brace.

I turned to find Avril wrestling with a bald Arab, who was also in tailored painter's duds. She was about to fail dramatically. I cut in like a jealous boyfriend and inhaled a lung full of his breath. It smelled like stale balloon air. I cradled his slippery head and felt my abdominals clench. I kneed him in the groin. He doubled over and began to shake. He was wearing a leg brace.

"What is the deal with these guys?"

Moustache Man was up again. And that's when I noticed him, a third person, a big white guy with stringy, gray hair and a matching beard. He was huge. Enormous. Built like a winner at the Muscle Show. He sprinted from a white Ford van, wearing two knee braces and an elbow strap.

"Kick his knees!" I shouted as I turned to deal with Moustache Man, and executed an impossibly long roundhouse kick that should have hamstrung me.

This time Moustache Man dropped like a puppet, and I missed. He lay in a pile of limbs, a position I'd never seen a human body perform. I halted, stupefied, and stared. Then he jumped up and struck my left temple. I didn't feel it, but two more like that and I would.

This is all wrong. People don't move like this.

I rushed him and jumped. I threw punches with no result; he moved to avoid them. Then he grabbed my jacket and yanked. I went down and all but kissed his soaking moustache. I spit. Then he rolled and got on top. He hit my nose and I felt it crack, but lightly as if through Novocain. I tasted blood and then started drinking.

Animal howled. Kairos invoked Kronos and staunched the flow.

Moustache Man was punching hard, making my head bounce off the pavement. Pain turned my hearing into a ringing phone. I was trying to block the blows but was succeeding less and less.

Then I had an idea, and I went with it. I aimed and Kairos corrected, sharpening imaginary crosshairs. With only a fraction of the force I'd been using, I let go a short-range jab and connected just below the sternum. It sent him down and into a palsy.

"Remember that! Hit the nerve clusters!" I announced.

I staggered up to find Avril strangling the third one, Big Gray Beard. She was tiny compared to him. He was lurching and she was flopping doll-like on his back, digging her fingers into his eyes. I was impressed when he went down, but this was still a two-man gig.

I leapt five feet and landed beside them on Animal-piloted legs. I tried to box him on the ear, but got rerouted. Instead, I struck opened-palmed at the spot where the skull and spine connect. I missed Avril by hairs.

Kairos, you're a surgeon!

Big Gray Beard fell down, quivering. That's all I had time to do before I had to rush forward and deal with Bald Arab again. Shit! These guys weren't normal! And I was quickly winding down.

I'd been hearing a noise for a while now, but only when I caught a glimpse of blue and red did I realize it was sirens. Cop tires smoked on the tarmac as Bald Arab did the signature puppet collapse. I checked behind me and confirmed what I already knew: the others were lying flat on their backs, playing dead.

"Fuuuck!" I blurted as the cops rushed the scene. I put my hands up and let them tackle me.

⊐7⊐?

Police custody is a nightmare. We lay flat on the street while seven huge cops held us at gun point and frisked us. A little overkill if you ask me, but then again, this was Detroit.

The ambulance siren wailed until someone killed the switch. Paramedics examined the three Painter Brothers and then loaded them up on gurneys and carted them off. They checked my nose and told me it was just bruised, then taped a cut and gave me some wet towels to clean off the blood. I was otherwise unscathed. Avril too. She had some bruises on her ribs, but nothing major.

When the paramedics finished with me the cops took over. I'd just killed three men. That's what the evidence said. Obvious, wasn't it? Once they did a pat down on Avril they stuffed her in a squad car. With me, however, not so nice. They wanted answers and they were nervous. For all they knew I was some kind of super soldier gone psycho.

Two cops bent me over the hood of a car and took turns shouting in my ear and shoving my face into their paint job. I wondered why the paramedics had bothered taping me up. Then they backed off in a hurry and pulled me up. That's when I saw the satellite mounted Channel 7 News cargo van. Can't have police brutality on primetime, you know.

Reporters are really obnoxious, almost as obnoxious as cops. Before this incident, I'd never known how much. The chick had all the hairspray in the world, but no shame. She kept shoving the mic into my face trying to wedge her way between the boys in blue. I laughed as they stuffed me into the backseat of the squad car.

I guess we put on quite a show.

Question was: who'd called them?

Δꟿⵝ⏽

"Self-defense," I said, "ever hear of it?"

"I don't like your attitude…uh, what's your name? Bradshaw?"

I exhaled at the prick in a suit. "I need a smoke."

He turned away and snapped his fingers to make some lackey run errands for the criminal. I'd already given them the name Edward Bradshaw. My ID said "Thomas Hunter," but I said I'd gotten it out of the safety deposit box because Thomas Hunter used to be Thomas Bradshaw, my twin brother.

I told him I didn't have my "real" ID because I'd left my wallet at the hotel bar and hoped it hadn't gone missing.

He gave me a cigarette and lit it. I took my sweet time enjoying it. I hated interrogations. I'd sat in on plenty myself, with Walser and the boys, playing the cool citizen with a police résumé.

I smacked my lips and looked at Detective Randall Schmidt of

Detroit PD. I exhaled. I was so tired.

"Now I need a cup a coffee."

He looked at me like he was going to shoot me.

"I'm wiped. That fight…you want me to talk or not?"

He snapped his fingers. I continued to smoke and let my gaze drift to the peeling green paint. I looked at the video camera in the upper corner of the room. I was pretty sure I looked like I was just smarting off, challenging male dominance. I wasn't. I was thinking. Carefully mulling over what I had already told him, what story I wanted to sell him next.

A story about crazy Satanists wouldn't hold water. I didn't believe it either. That this had also happened to me back home wasn't something I wanted them to know about. I realized I probably had a bench warrant in California for failure to appear.

I understood my enemy's MO now: send shaved-headed cultist for a fight and, when the cops come, lay a "dead" body at my feet. I'd bet ten to one that the guy who put a brick through my window was sitting in Walser's morgue as fresh as the day he dropped.

If one didn't get me a conviction, four surely would.

Avril's words came back and bit. *The minute we start looking for where that key goes, we're on the clock.* Somebody or some*thing* wanted me out of the way, and I wanted to know who or what that was.

I was halfway through the shitty coffee when Schmidt put his fist on the table and leaned into it.

"You're gonna talk now," he said. "I'm gonna press record and then you're gonna explain things to my satisfaction, get it?"

"Are you arresting me or not?" I said, yawning and blinking away tears of exhaustion, buying more time, but also subtly reminding him of the rules. He wasn't going to arrest me. I already knew that. While he would say he had enough probable cause to throw my ass in jail, he didn't really, as long as he didn't find out about the incident back home. But he could get me on resisting arrest if I didn't cooperate. He was hoping I would keep mouthing off so he could do that. If I wanted to outwit the demon and his bald-headed Satanists, I would have to chill out and give him enough of what he wanted to let me walk. Today anyway.

Right now he had my word and Avril's. Our stories would parallel each other. They'd have to go through the motions and get other witness statements too, if they wanted to press charges. They wouldn't want to do all that work.

He pushed record.

I told him all about my brother, about the safety deposit box. I showed him the key as proof. I detailed the entire journey, from when I first met Avril, all the way forward to our fight with the three painters. I explained that I believed them to have heart conditions and other terminal illnesses based on their multiple braces and strange seizures. It was my attempt to explain why they'd dropped dead like that.

That was the weakest part of my monologue, but I couched it all in the language of victimization and self-defense and the lie that I feared Avril might be pregnant so that my total intent had been to protect her and my unborn child.

I told him to check the bank for an attestation of my innocence. Whether they could do that or not I didn't care, I wanted to show honest connection with a reputable institution. Then I produced a white card with an address written on it, the only thing I'd gotten from the safety deposit box.

"This is what they were after, I think. I have no idea why."

He took the card from me and read the address. He tossed it on the table and said, "Wait here. I'll be back."

Now was the time to get with the other cops so they could all discuss what to do. A couple of minutes later, he walked back in the room.

"You can go."

I pushed the chair back, but before I stood up he said, "Don't think for a minute that this is over. I'm not authorizing you to leave the state. If I find you have any prior involvement or affiliation with these guys, even so much as members at the same Bingo hall, I'll have you trussed up on first degree murder charges faster than you can say 'Bingo was his name-o.' You get me?"

"Yes, sir," I said.

"The officer on duty will drive you back to your car. Where is it, the bank?"

149

"Bingo," I said.

Avril was waiting for me. "Let's get the fuck out of here."

We had no time to dally over our misfortunes.

The minute we start looking for where that key goes, we're on the clock.

We got safely back to our rental car, and I set a course for the address on the card: Missionary Baptist Church on East Warren, Rev. Samuel Williams. *Come Pray with Me.*

"Was he Christian, this Edward?"

"Yeah," she said. "Like Judas."

We were racing the sun, my exhaustion and the crazy Satanists, who were surely organizing for another bout of entrapment. The fight had done a number on me. Not the injuries, but the recovery. The circles under my eyes were a nasty, dark purple. My nose wasn't broken, or if it had been, it wasn't anymore.

Energy wise I was in bad shape. Pain is good for a caveman who doesn't know that fire is hot yet. For me, pain just slows me down. I can feel the impact without the setback, so I could fight three crazy painters in back braces all at once. But when it was done, I was on a fast sinking spiral into unconsciousness. I figured I had about thirty minutes before I collapsed.

"Coffee!" I pointed to an empty drive-through.

Dusk had come already, but I really didn't want to spend another night in Detroit.

"We have no more room for fuck-ups," Avril said as I chugged a venti.

"If we see any more big guys with bald heads I say we run the other way."

"Agreed."

Warren Avenue brought with it a host of tumbledown houses and loiterers, most of them wearing baggy pants and combs in their hair. A couple of white people in a rental seemed to catch their interest a little too much.

"Park there," I said, pointing to a spot about half a block away from a group of three. I wasn't afraid of these hoodlums, but I surely didn't need to tempt fate.

We walked quickly across the street to the brick church. It had old, beaten up trim and a kiosk sign that didn't light and read: *Did God leave Detroit or did Detroit leave God?*

"I'd say a little bit of both."

The door was open and, with a sigh of relief, we stepped inside.

"Who are we looking for again?" she asked.

"Reverend Williams."

"Well, yo in luck then." The voice came from…somewhere.

Don't like this place, Boss.

"Reverend Williams!" I proclaimed. I didn't see anyone; I was just talking to the same air that had greeted us. Then slowly, a figure began to march from the altar.

As Reverend Williams came closer, I could see the cane and the hitched stride of a thin black man, old as Moses.

"It is I!" he said. "Now the only question is, who is you?"

"Sir," I nodded. "My name is Thomas Hunter and this is Avril."

"Nice to meet you, Thomas Hunter. And nice to meet you, Ms. Avril. Now, what can I do for you?"

"I have your card," I said and pulled the wrinkled thing out of my pocket.

He laughed. "You sho do," he said. "Will you look at that?" I opened my mouth to reply but he cut me off. "You should know, which you may not, that I don't give these out very often."

"You're right. I didn't know that."

"I know you didn't," he said, "because I didn't give that to you. If I had, I would remember yo face."

"I'm sure that—"

"However, I do remember yo face, but I know yo face is not the face I remember. If that makes any sense to you."

"Kind of."

"In other words, you look like Edward Bradshaw, but you ain't. Am I right?"

I paused. He was good. "Yes, sir, that's correct."

"I know it is," he said. "Now the only question that remains is, why?" And when he said "why" he said it "whhhy." Then we looked at each other for a while and I was pretty sure we were the only two people in the universe. Avril watched us and said nothing. Apparently, this was my part in all this. This was why she'd needed me: to get past the gatekeeper at journey's end.

"Well," he said, "I do believe that I am ready for a cup of very dark, very good coffee. And I'll just bet that you are, too!"

We followed him through the chapel to a door behind the altar and up a narrow wooden stairway into a cozy alcove. The monk in me smiled.

"You can have a seat in those two chairs right there." He pointed to a couple of Civil War era parlor chairs across from a worn couch. The coffee table in between held more than one rickety tower of books and Bibles. In the far corner sat a kitchenette, where he was already breaking out the coffee.

Avril and I sat down in the chairs and gave each other odd looks.

"Go ahead," he called over his shoulder. "Go ahead and move some of those books to the floor if you would. It'll just take me a second here to make it just the way I think yo gonna love it. Doo-dah, doo-dah."

I made a face at Avril to make her laugh. "A nice place you have here," I called out.

"Oh, well, thank you. I make do. I make do. And in today's world that's not such an easy thing to do. Camp-town ladies sing this song, doo-dah, doo-dah!"

"You got that right."

He came over with a silver serving tray, cups, sugar and cream. Avril jumped up to take it from him, but he simply said, "Oh, that's just fine. I might walk with a cane when I leave here, but I'll be danged if I can't walk across my livin' room all by myself! Now sit, young lady."

He set the service down slowly on the table where we'd cleared off the books. Then he repeated the whole show once the coffee was done, singing Camp Town Races under his breath. We doctored up our coffees and then sipped gingerly.

"Well?" he said. "How'd I do?"

I shifted in my seat. "You make a perfect cup."

"Thank you."

We drank our coffee and didn't talk for a minute. Then he said, "Well, I suppose we should get down to business, don't you?"

I nodded. "Agreed. But I don't know what that business is."

"Fair enough," he said. "Fortunately for you, I do."

"Well then, lead the way, sir."

"The Lord works in sta-range and unnatural ways sometimes," he said, the sermon in his voice coming naturally. "Folks like to say he works in 'mysterious ways,' but you'll not find that anywhere in the Bible. So, I say 'sta-range and unnatural.' Not always, but sometimes, you understand?

"Now, I don't care if you believe in God or Jesus or the Devil himself, because if you don't that don't make it any less real to me, but I think you'll agree there is enough strange and unnatural business occurring in this world that the idea of God isn't so farfetched as some folks might want to believe."

"Makes sense," I said. He held up the palm of his hand and shook his head. He went on.

"There's power, Mr. Hunter. Ms. Avril. Power of all kinds. Good, evil and in between. I seen this power before. And I know you have too, Mr. Hunter." He swallowed with such a dry click in his throat it made me want to drink a glass of water. "You may sometimes ask yourself whhy do things happen the way they do? Whhy, this or that? Well, I can tell ya, everything has a reason. I say that as a matter of course. Everything has action and reaction. Cause and effect. Yin and yang. We create the world we live in. Do you understand? There is energy and there is how we use it.

"You can always find the whhy's and whherefores. You can always explain a mystery. And you can always find somethin' that's lost, if you know where to look."

At this point I wasn't sure if this was going anywhere. In fact, I was pretty sure it wasn't. I believed this old preacher here just needed someone to talk to. He'd probably met my brother and invited him up for coffee in just this same fashion and—Avril tapped my arm.

"Look." She nodded toward the other room.

I looked, saw the corner of a neatly made bed.

"The window," she said.

I looked at the window in the other room. "Yeah?"

Avril stood up and walked over to it. That's when I noticed Reverend Williams had stopped talking. He was just sitting there pleasantly smiling. What punch line had I missed?

I followed after Avril. We stared out the window together.

"What is it?" I asked, and then I read the sign on the front lawn. "Wayne County Medical Examiner—the morgue. Oh, shit."

"Edward's dead," Avril said.

"Ah, Reverend," I called out, "are we supposed to go into the morgue here?" And then under my breath added, "If it's even open."

"You'll find that doors open to the right-e-us," Reverend Williams said from behind us. "Go and find that which is lost."

"Oh, whoa. I gotta sit down." The room had begun spinning. I took a deep breath. "Coffee just ran out," I gasped. "I need water."

"Sit down on that bed there, I'll fetch you some water with lemon." The Reverend walked over with a glass already in hand. I finished it in three easy gulps, but to my luck, he'd brought more than one. Had I noticed that before? I got halfway through the second glass before handing it off to Avril.

"I'm sorry…it's…I'm so tired…"

Darkness. The world slipped away as I dove down into the healing slumber that always follows use of my increased stamina.

ך ֿה ֿ-ן ֿך

When I woke up it was morning. Gray morning. Detroit morning. The light cast a filmy haze over the room, gray, so gray. And dust. And…I sat up.

"Huh? Avril?" I called out. "Avril!"

It was all wrong, the whole apartment. Nothing was the same. It seemed I'd been taken somewhere, moved, but…the layout was familiar. The bed in the corner, the window, and outside it, the Wayne County Medical Examiner.

"What the…? Reverend?"

No answer. And it was cold, much colder than it had been the night before. I got up, naked but for my underwear. I heard the latch click, and the door whining on rusty hinges. I braced for… *something*.

I exhaled when Avril came in.

"Oh, Thomas, I'm sorry!" She hugged me and together we sat on the bed. She kissed me. "You okay now? I thought you were going to sleep longer, so I went out. I'm sorry. But I got you something."

154

She brought in a large coffee and a bear claw. I normally don't eat that stuff, the bear claw that is. I devoured it in seconds. I needed energy. I gulped the coffee.

"Where—wh-what the hell?" I stammered. The place was a mess, a total disaster. There was thick dust everywhere, springs were sticking out of the furniture. Paint was peeling and hanging in strips a foot wide, or bubbling across the ceiling like old scars.

"I thought there'd been a fire," she said, "but nothing's burned."

I walked into the living room, to the chairs we'd sat in the night before, which were now threadbare and covered in cobwebs. The books on the coffee table rotted in their bindings. Those we'd moved to the floor lay scattered in dust as if we'd laid them there half a century ago, except for one. It grabbed my attention. The center of the cover cut a square outline where dust had not accumulated, like a shoveled patch in deep snow. Something had been removed.

"What happened?" she asked.

I glared at her. "Don't act like that. God, how could I have been so duped? I'm losing my touch, man."

"Excuse me?"

"Just stop it, okay? You know exactly what happened here, so don't act like you don't know. I'm not playing this game with you anymore. Just acknowledge what I'm saying and move on." I was getting the shakes, a slow-acting rage response. I couldn't even look at her.

Animal began muttering.

"Acknowledged," she said.

"Good! Now, was that so hard? Thank you for being truthful for once." I was ready to smack her. I just needed her to stop feigning ignorance. She knew damn well what had made the Reverend disappear and why this space had become covered in years-old dust.

"Eddy was a Grand Master." "Thank you. A Grand Master of what? What discipline, because I have never known anyone to have that kind of control."

"Anyone?"

"No. I'm the best I know of, but I can't even come close to what your precious fucking *Eddy* did here. So, dare I ask what trap are you planning to lead me into next?"

"You're jealous."

I reached for my clothes and shrugged. "This guy can totally wrap you around his finger and lay a trick the likes of which God would have trouble with."

"Yeah, he's also dead," she said, pointing to the morgue outside.

"How is it dead when they can come back to life and throw punches?"

"What are you talking about?"

"Admit it!"

"What are you saying, that I had something to do with those guys who attacked us yesterday? Those painters?"

"Does the shoe fit?"

"What?" she rasped.

"Does. The. Shoe. Fit?"

"Are you for real?"

I shrugged.

"You think I'm leading you to your death, don't you? You think after coming all this way, fucking you night after night, that I'm literally leading you"—she pointed out the window at the morgue—"to what? Switch bodies in there? Put you in the tray and walk out with Eddy?"

"Is that an admission of guilt?"

Apparently that was the wrong thing to say, because she screamed. She screamed at the top of her lungs, and then she screamed at the bottom of them. Then just screamed.

"You have no right!" she bawled, tears streaming from her eyes. "No fucking right!" She dropped to her knees and wept.

I stood there, shame burning my cheeks. I'd been wrong. She wasn't trying to hurt me. She wasn't playing me. She wasn't leading me to my death. She was helping me, protecting me. And she was the only one I could trust.

"Oh, God." I went to her, wrapped my arms around her and refused to let go until she stopped fighting me. I held her while she sobbed.

"I'm sorry," I whispered.

אכ ב ﬞ

In terms of Old World arcana and ghost magick, Edward had done the equivalent of making the Statue of Liberty disappear. I'd called it a trap because I didn't trust my elusive brother, and I had been suspicious of Avril's intent. Okay, fine, I was jealous.

Sometimes when you know a bit about an art or science, you run into someone who practices it in a manner that mere mortals can only dream of. Like Tesla with his wireless electricity in the nineteenth century.

What Edward had done in the case of the good Reverend Williams was set up a Gate Guardian who could not only impress full visual, olfactory and tactile effects in real time on living beings, but also show up on cue for the exact right person. And make a good cup of coffee to boot. This was the equivalent of doing a backflip while drinking a glass of water and, at the same time, making a sandwich. Without leaving any crumbs behind.

Now, any spiritmancer like myself can get a ghost to do his bidding. I don't like to do it. I guess because I feel it's unfair, but Edward apparently thought nothing of it. He'd gotten the ghost of Reverend Williams to haunt his parish inside out, and I mean that in the most literal sense. Instead of seeing the energetic imprint of the ghost, what I call the Medallion, one saw the ghost's whole vision inside his spacetime as if it were one's own spacetime. The ghost's universe became *the* universe. So we'd seen it as Williams had.

He'd basically worked a trick to make the equivalent of a holodeck style haunted house.

I was in awe.

I knew what he'd done; I just had no clue how he'd done it. It could take a lifetime to figure out a trick like that. I stopped trying when we got to the morgue.

⟨﹏�᠎⟩

The pimple-faced attendant at the front desk wasn't all that interested in his job. It took a while for us to get in front of someone who could open the crypt. Finally, a huge black guy by the name of Bigboy stepped through the door.

"Bigboy, they need to get into the crypt."

Bigboy looked at me like he was sizing me up for a meal.

"Was'up?"

"Hi, Bigboy. I'm Thomas. My brother went missing in Detroit, and I'm pretty sure he's dead, so I wanted to check here. You must have some unidentified bodies, right?"

"Oh, yeah!" he said. "Hell yeah. Man, they ain't gave us nuthin' down here from State. Sheeeit, body's pilin' up like it the end a the world. Sheeeit!"

"Really?"

"Yeah really. Oh, man. Sixty-eight a them mo' fuckers up in here! Can you belieeeve dat shit? Nobody claim 'em. Folk so poor in this mo fuckin' town, they cain't even afford to burry they own dead. And we so po' we cain't even burn 'em! Shit's worse than nineteenth century London, man! Sheeeit!

"Know what I mean? How the hell you gonna run a goddamn morgue when you cain't burry or burn them mo' fuckin' dead bodies? Come on, man."

We followed him through a series of doors and drab looking corridors before reaching a big, metal door with a square, glass porthole. Bigboy peeked inside.

"There they is." He laughed. "Man, if I was a gravedigger, I be all up in this shit, man. You know I would! Daaamn!"

Bigboy stepped aside, and I took a look. Rows of body bags, crusted with ice, lined the floor. It made me think of bags of frozen peas.

"So, sixty-eight dead bodies in there? Is that what the clerk said?"

"Frozen like popsicles. How the hell you gonna find yo brother, up in here? You gonna open up every one a those ziplock bags and look at them frozen ass faces a all them niggas?"

I took a deep breath. "Do I have a choice?"

"Do you have a choice? Maaan, you always got a choice!"

"Like?"

"Walk the fuck away. Hahaha, man. Jus' kiddin'." Then Bigboy's face dropped to deadpan serious and a dark pall came over all of us. I looked into those big, brown eyes and knew he'd been acting the ignorant fool this whole time.

"Why don't you tell me what he look like and maybe I already know where he is," he said in a low, careful voice. He sounded like a young Barry White.

"Okay. He looks like me," I said, remembering the smooth access granted me at the bank to Edward's accounts.

"Thank you. Then we done here. Follow me if you don't mind."

We walked elsewhere, away from the walk-in refrigerator, past the drawers, into another room, where silence made its home. Four quarter-block, stainless steel doors lined the walls in here, sixteen doors total. To my surprise, Bigboy pulled out a ring of keys and began unlocking the door.

"This where we keep da special shit," he said, putting his big, black hand on a knob and staring at me. "Like motherfuckers who don't decompose."

⊐7◻꒭

"Twins? Can't be. We were born years apart and in different cities." We stood around the open tray. Me, Avril, Bigboy and Animal, who'd been saying over and over again, *don't look, don't look, don't look!*

"I didn't realize how much you look like him," said Avril, dry-eyed now.

I shook my head. "I didn't always look like him."

"No," she agreed, "not like this."

"What the frick, Boss? How—will you shut up!"

"You all right, Mr. Hunter?"

"Yes. Bigboy, I'm fine. Better than fine. Thank you."

We stood in silence—sweet, sweet silence—staring at the naked body on the tray. Even down to the musculature, this was my body, a doppelganger. Eerie.

"Okay," I said, "he's an Incorruptible, that's what I needed to know. And we found him, which I guess was the whole point of all this, right?" I looked at Avril.

She swallowed thickly and said, "He's dead."

I didn't respond. I wasn't sure why she would make such a seemingly obvious remark.

"Thomas, we have to cremate."

"What?"

"You heard me. We have to cremate. Now."

"No. No, he's—"

"Hunter, he's dead."

"Not like normal, he ain't. No."

She stared at me, incredulous. "Look!"

She picked his arm up and let it flop. Tears were collecting in the corners of her eyes.

I shook my head in defiance, then began counting on my fingers.

"No rigor mortis. No putrefaction. No saponification. No decay. No odor. What kind of death do you call this?"

No one said anything. I went on. "Because it's not death. It's—it's another trick."

"Thomas, no! He's dead. We end this. Right now." The tears were streaming from her eyes.

I looked at her in utter disbelief, and then all the little fragmented clues came together.

"You came all this way with me, just to cremate *him*?"

She didn't respond. She blinked. Wiped tears.

Boss, it's the first thing she done that's right!

"But why?" I begged.

"Baby…" she reached for me.

"No!" I stabbed my finger out between us. "Don't fucking 'baby' me. Just answer me. Why?"

Boss…

"Shh! Why?" And when she didn't answer, I shouted at her. "Stop hiding things from me!"

She gritted her teeth and stared me down, eyes red-rimmed. "To end it!" she seethed. "To end all of *this!*"

"What is *this*, for the last fucking time?"

"The end of *everything*," she breathed. "Edward is the key. Don't you get it? Not just a safety deposit box, but a clue. Not just a body, but a pathway. He left it here, locked away and hidden, so that we—you and I—could come and destroy it before they got hold of it. The enemy—those people that have been chasing us around, chasing you, want this thing!" She pointed at the body. "They have to have this thing. You understand? You must burn it."

"Oh, and there you go again," I mumbled, "knowing so much

and telling so little."

"I don't know everything there is to know about it," she rasped, "but I know that the less you know, the better off you are.

"It's a criminal underground with more connections to government and higher circles than you could ever dream of. They practice black magick, okay? They sacrifice people, adults and children; they practice cannibalism, okay? Do I need to say more? They drink blood. They keep slaves. They eat brains, baptize with urine. They're bad people, Hunter. Some are not even people at all."

I shook my head, and then I burst into mad giggles. Was I supposed to believe her? Crazy, criminal conspiracies. But it was what she'd said. The minute she tells me anything, I think she's lying. Or crazy.

I rubbed my eyes with the heels of my hands.

"Oh, God."

"Hunter, trust me on this. We have to burn it!"

Burn it, Boss!

"Shut the hell up, Animal!"

"Mr. Hunter, with all due respect and shit like that, we cremate for under eight hundred dollah—"

"Thank you, Bigboy. That is not—I'm not worried about the cost."

"Then what is your problem?" Avril demanded.

"All this talk about how much you love him and now you come here just to burn him? What the hell is wrong with you?"

"This is so hard for me, you have no idea. You can't know the pain I feel. I loved him so much, Hunter. I'm sorry, but it's true. I don't want to do it anymore than you do. I don't want to let go either, but I have to, because it's not about me. Or you. It's about something so much bigger, something that must be stopped."

I shook my head. I didn't want to acknowledge what she was saying. I didn't want to listen.

"The body—it's not dead," I said.

"Mr. Hunter, he dead—"

"Not the normal way," I said.

I couldn't let it go. I hadn't expected this at all, but seeing him lying there an Incorruptible, looking like me, I couldn't do it. My mind searched for a subterfuge. I turned to Bigboy.

"Then why do you have a lock on the door? You don't have locks on any other doors. What do you think's going to happen?"

"Sheeeit, man. I don't know."

I turned to Avril. "What?"

She was shaking her head at me. Then she let out a breathy laugh.

"I don't believe it," she said.

"What don't you believe?"

"You."

"Why?"

"It's the trick, isn't it?"

I shook my head. "I don't know what you're talking about."

She chuckled madly. "Yes, you do. You egotistical sonovabitch. He one upped you in that apartment. That was bad enough, but this—" She pointed at the body again.

I shook my head and took a deep breath.

"What she talkin' about, Mr. Hunter?"

"What I'm talking about, Bigboy," said Avril, without taking her eyes off me, "is the fact that Mr. Hunter's brother here is a better wizard than Mr. Hunter and Mr. Hunter can't fucking stand it."

"And," I said sharply, "what does that have to with anything?"

"It's the trick," she said. "*This* trick. You don't know how he or those painters or Satanists do it, but you have to find out. You won't let it rest until you do, you stubborn, stupid asshole."

I shrugged. Blinked. Sucked my teeth.

"Well?" she said.

"Well, I don't know what to say. You're right. I'm going to find out how he did the Williams thing and how he's doing this thing. I will. And when I do, I will go and find the beginning of this whole mess and shut it down. If what you say is true, then—"

"That's not how you shut it down," she said. "You shut it down by burning this body right here in this tray."

I shook my head. "No. I shut it down my way. I'll learn the trick, and I'll find the source. That's my method. They want this body, they'll come after it."

"You'll end up in jail or worse."

I shrugged. "I'll use Walser. I'll get a pardon. I'll kick my way out."

"Thomas, you can't always kick your way out of things."

"So far, so good."

"You don't know the first thing about what you're saying. You don't know this game you're playing!"

"Then tell me!" I stared at her for too long. "Yeah see, you won't."

"I told you what I know."

"Unless you can tell me something that I can use, I am going to do what I think I should. My way."

She shook her head. She was wrestling with herself.

"You won't be able to resist it, Hunter. Once you find out how these things are done, these tricks, the power, the—it'll take over. It will corrupt you."

"Interesting choice of words," I said.

"Damn it, Hunter!"

"I'm doing this," I said.

"No. No, I won't let you." She got between me and the body.

"Knock it off!"

"You don't know what you're doing."

"I know what I'm doing. Bigboy."

The big, black man shook his head. "Man, you all got some fucked up lives."

Avril stood poised like a traffic mom guarding a kid crossing. I thought about it. She was shaking her head. I sighed. Then made a show of looking down at the floor and brooding.

"Fine. Fuck it. Let's go. Bigboy, let me give you my credit card number."

"Oh, let's get the form, man. Got to have you fill out the release."

"Lead the way."

The three of us gathered in an office, which was so cluttered that papers were slopping off the desk onto the floor and piling up the wall.

"Oh, shit," I said.

"What?"

"I think I left my wallet in the car."

"It's not in your back pocket?" Avril asked.

"No, I think I put it in the glove box." I held out the keys to her.

She snatched the keys and stepped out of the room. I listened to her heels click down the hall.

I pulled my wallet out of an inner jacket pocket.

"Okay, Bigboy, I want my brother transferred to San Francisco."

"Maaan, I knew you was pullin' some kin' a—."

"That's fuckin' right, Bigboy. Don't say a word. There's plenty of money in it for you."

"I ain't no nineteenth century body hawker!"

"No. But you are a twenty-first century Detroit citizen. Couple grand would go a long way, I'm guessing. Eh? How 'bout it? Lot's a fried—"

"Watch yo mouth, son."

"You know what I mean, Bigboy. How about a couple?"

"A couple what?"

"A couple grand."

"Like five," he said.

"Five? Five? Bigboy, now…"

He started shaking his head. "Maaan, you got no idea how hard times been up in this place. Mo' fuckah's stealing all kinds a shit. Copper piping. Fuckin' church gold. Old lady rings. Mothah fuckah's will take yo mothah fuckin' iPhone right out yo mothah fuckin hand. I need *in*surance, man. I figure fi' gran' probably buy me dat."

I glanced back through the crack in the door. Suddenly I was worried that I'd sent Avril to the street by herself. I had to wrap this up. I leaned toward him and spoke in a harsh whisper.

"This is fuckin' highway robbery, Bigboy! You ought to be ashamed of yourself, you know that? Ashamed. A lot of people are going to be interested in this, so if I give you five thousand fucking dollars I expect you to come through, okay?"

"My word," he said with his hand over his heart.

"Okay, five Gs. You got it."

"Plus we don't normally transfer cadavers, Mr. Hunter."

"Fine! Six Gs. Fuck, Bigboy, help me out here. Six fuckin' Gs and—"

"How I'm gonna get it?"

"You ship the body and you get the money. It's that easy. But look, here." I pulled out a blank check I kept on hand for emergencies. My fingers were shaking. Avril would be back any minute. "Give me that pen." My fingers clenched. Conscience. "Fuuuuck!" I bit my lip and forced my hand. I managed to scribble out a shaky, kindergarten level script "$3,000.00" and shoved it at him. "Now take it! Take the fuckin' money. You get the rest when I get the body! Here's a business card!"

"Paranormal Investigator?"

"Yes!"

The door opened.

"Anyway, what did you say it was gonna be?" I said like a game show host, looking up into Avril's eyes as she stepped back into the office.

"It wasn't in there," she said, annoyed.

"Yeah. Sorry, babe, it was in my jacket pocket all along. Anyway, you said—"

"Eleven hundred," said Bigboy.

I nodded. "Eleven hundred for bur—"

"Cremation, Mr. Hunter."

"Cremation. Right. Okay, so here just take these digits down." I gave him my credit card number.

Avril and I didn't speak on the way to the airport. We watched for errant painters and otherwise hidden attackers. Once inside the airport, I worried that we'd be on some list of fleeing criminals and get flagged as soon as we checked in. It didn't happen.

Once we got past the x-ray machines, I chilled out. Somehow the idea of reanimated Incorruptibles coming after us while we were in the airport seemed ludicrous. They didn't like witnesses as much as they liked the appearance of the police.

I found Avril sitting by the window reading a book she'd purchased from the gift shop. She didn't look up as I sat down.

I sort of wondered if this was it between her and I. Sad and strange. Our relationship had not turned out how I'd expected. Then again, whose does? I loved her. I can say that. But, fire and ice, or probably more like fire and fire, the two of us. I watched her as she drank her coffee and read her book, the fine features of her face, her delicate and untamed beauty.

I would see Walser personally about the body of my Incorruptible brother. I didn't want to risk sending an email or even making a phone call. I felt watched, monitored. We boarded the plane, and I got a window seat. Avril read her book, and I wanted to kiss her. I wanted to say I was sorry for all the things I'd said, my accusations and distrust. But I didn't, because I still didn't trust her. She had... lied? No, concealed her true purpose from me. She had not wanted to admit her interest was one of destruction. I wondered if she had known all along about Edward's fate. If she'd known he was dead all the while. It had been her, after all, who'd spotted the Wayne County Morgue through Williams' open window, and she'd worked it out too quickly.

Or maybe I'd just been too slow.

I ordered a drink. Then another and another. The flight went longer than I thought it should. They always do. By the time we touched down, I was seeing double. I waited for the announcement and then turned on my phone. Three missed calls. All from... Bigboy?

I listened to the voicemail.

When I'd finished listening, I hung up and stared forward. Sweat began to pour from my brow. I clenched my teeth and then ground them. The seats in front of me lurched back and forth. The fuselage was spinning even though we weren't moving.

"Who was it?" Avril asked, the first time she'd spoken to me since the morgue.

I shook my head. "I don't know."

"You don't know? Thomas, who was it?"

Everyone was standing now. We were getting off. I thought I was going to vomit. I squeezed my fingers into a fist and punched the seat in front of me.

"Thomas!"

"I don't know." I was breathing heavily and seeing red through a haze of alcohol.

"Oh my God, you're shitfaced!"

The people in front were getting their bags out of the overhead compartments. Some had begun to stare at us, at me. I drained the last of my drink and shoved the plastic cup into the seat pouch in front of me. It broke and splintered in my hand.

"Thomas, who was it?"

I shook my head. "Yeah," I said, getting my bag. I stumbled out into the moving line. I burped and tasted acid.

I wasn't straight. I'd gotten too drunk. Me, too drunk. Avril was on my heels, she was prodding me for an answer.

"Who fucking called?" We were making a huge scene by now.

I just kept shaking my head and walking, stumbling. I couldn't admit to this. I couldn't believe what had just happened, what was happening.

"Oh, God," I passed the stewardess and ignored her Texan smile. I tripped in the ramp. "Animal!" I shouted, the incoherent ramblings of a drunk. "Animal!" I feared for what might happen in the next hours, the next minutes. I wanted to be armed and ready, but I was drunk…drunk with my crew fast asleep inside me.

And I had failed. I had thought the prize was mine, that I had been in control.

I pushed my way through offended travelers into the Santa Rosa airport. People everywhere. People staring, pointing. I checked them like the opposing team in a hockey game. I was stumbling and sweating and looking them all up and down, searching for back braces and knee straps.

I had underestimated my enemy. I had been wrong.

"Oh, fuck!" I breathed. Avril was lost somewhere behind me. I tripped and fell. I struck the floor. "Help!" I was crying. I had been so wrong. So stupid. It seemed like everyone turned at the same time and just stared at me. "What are you looking at?" But I knew what they were looking at: the wretched drunk on the ground, the drunk on his hands and knees, bags sprawled around him, dripping sweat and crying. I couldn't move. I curled into a ball and bawled. Pathetic drunk, bum and ghost hunter extraordinaire, Thomas Hunter.

"Help me!" *I should have burned him. I should have fucking burned him!* "Help me!"

Edward had come back to life.

Chapter 16

Security called the medics, who came running. They hauled me up off the floor and plopped me into a plastic seat, mopping my forehead and checking my vitals. This went on way too long. I stared at a little girl, who watched me as they took my blood pressure and listened to my heart.

"Heavily intoxicated with a panic attack," I overheard them say to Avril. "I would take him down to County to sober up if he wasn't with you. Hey, isn't he the—"

"No," she said.

"Oh. I'm sorry. Anyway, just see to it that he gets a good night's sleep and lays off the alcohol for a while."

"Thank you, I will."

△⊩☒ⵏ

"Mr. Hunter. Mr. Hunter. I got somethin' I gots to tell ya. I swear I don't know how, but…I mean, I don't know how to say what I'm about to say, but, uh…uh, sheeeit man, yo mothah fuckin' brother…he-he disappear. I mean, he…I turn around and I was gettin' the…the bag ready for shippin' and when I turn back around h-he gone. I mean, gone. I ran out and I look around, but I didn't see no one, man. I don't know how far a naked white man can get on his own in De-troit, but sheeeit!

I listened to it on speaker then erased it. Avril stared at me, no expression. Then she looked down and the disappointment, the disgust and the pity—that was the worst one—just seeped out of her.

We were sitting in the airport, and I was sobering up. I wasn't as drunk as I was panicked. I hadn't been able to say anything to her, fully expecting her to leave me here. To part company forever.

"You can go. I won't blame you."

She shook her head. "I'm afraid I have nowhere *to* go," she said.

"Then we should go back to Detroit and find him."

She shook her head. "I don't think so." She closed her eyes, and I watched them flutter as two tears slid from them. "Thomas, I don't know how to put this, but anywhere we go now, anyplace at all, will not be safe. Anyone could be involved. Anyone's a potential attacker. Everyone's a potential threat."

"To what? Kill us?"

She shook her head. "To use us. You. They want your crew, Hunter."

"Huh?"

"He wants your crew."

I laughed. "Who, Eddie? How could anyone possibly want this band of misfit entities?"

Avril shook her head. Then she took a deep breath and looked at me.

"No. Not Eddie. *Thomas Bradshaw.*"

"You mean me?"

"No. You're Thomas Hunter. Thomas Bradshaw is someone else entirely, a very bad man."

I tried to respond and fell short.

"Let's go." She stood up.

"Whoa, where are you going? And what the hell are you saying?"

"Hunter, come on!"

She was walking so fast I had to run to catch up.

"What are you doing?"

She held out her hand. "Give me your keys."

"What?"

"Give me your keys. You're drunk, and I can drive stick."

"I'm not drunk."

"Give."

"Be careful."

"I wasn't kidding. Or downplaying," she said. "We have to go, now."

I grabbed her arm and made her stop. "What did you mean back there, about saying *Thomas Bradshaw* would come looking for us."

"Hunter, I will tell you, okay. You're right that I've been very scarce with my information, and I'm sorry. I had to know what had happened for myself. I have a pretty good idea now. So, I will tell you, once we get out of here and some place safe. I will tell you the whole story. I promise."

"Fine. What do we do now?"

"Once we get outside, we sprint to the car. I mean it. Sprint and scream. Maximal disturbance."

I headed toward baggage claim. She caught my arm and hauled me toward the doors.

"Get ready!"

We burst out of the Charles Schultz Airport and bolted through wandering travelers. I knocked over a shrieking lady. I started to double back, but abandoned the idea. I raced past the two horribly ugly bronze statues of Linus and Lucy.

Then Avril started screaming.

"Animal, you awake?"

Yeah, Boss.

"Now's your chance: howl!"

It was a pretty sick sounding howl. Not nearly canine enough, a sort of drunken caveman yawp.

We sprinted over the lawns and paved medians to the Box. Avril clicked the doors opened as we barreled toward it. We got inside and collapsed.

"Do…you…think…we scared…off…the Satanists with…that shit?"

"I have an idea of where to go." Avril floored it, turning corners like Tron. She took the 101 freeway and hauled. She merged into the fast lane and brought our speed up to eighty, eighty-five, ninety.

Traffic had died off hours ago, and the road was clear. I saw lights flash behind us and heard sirens.

"Oh, shit, we're being pulled over!"

"No," she breathed. "Can't risk it." She pressed on the accelerator.

I slumped in my seat, my mind racing. Did we really need to risk a high-speed chase in the name of fleeing from some crazy conspiracy? I thought about half a dozen possibilities, all of which involved me doing illegal things to police officers.

"Is that an ambulance behind us?"

"Huh?" I turned around. A Super Duty Ford van was barreling down the freeway, gaining on us. Some part of me sighed relief. Not cops, medics! But that elation quickly gave way to another realization. *Why send an ambulance?*

That's when the wheel listed to the right and Avril slumped forward. Comatose.

"Holy fuck!"

The small car careened into an oncoming vehicle. A horn blared. I grabbed the wheel and yanked, inches from collision, but it was an overcompensation and the car lurched the other way. The tires screeched, and I smelled the stink of burning rubber.

"Animal!"

Kairos was calculating away, but things were happening too fast. The Box entered a dangerous zigzagging slalom at eighty miles per hour, while I frantically tried to steady it.

"I can't hold it, Boss!"

The car wasn't slowing. When I'd nudged Avril to get at the steering wheel, she had flopped to the side but, impossibly, her foot had stayed heavy on the gas peddle.

I looked up into blinding headlights. A semi truck's horn wailed. I cranked the wheel again and cleared the front end, but not the rear. The truck nailed the driver's side and sent us spinning like a Matchbox car. I grabbed the stick shift and yanked it back. The Box bucked like a stallion and sailed into the guard rail. Metal folded. Glass shattered, and then…then the lights went out.

I'd had my car accident after all.

Chapter 17

Boss? Boss?

Animal…

Yeah, Boss, got your back.

Damages?

Nothin' we can't take care of.

Estimate?

A couple months.

What?

I mean days, Boss. A couple days. Sorry, Kronos is hard to read down there. He's slipping more and more inside.

I opened my eyes, or thought I did, and saw a haze of light.

"No need to worry, we'll have you cured soon."

"Can you…see anything…wait—" *what did you say?* The voice had not been familiar.

"You're with loved ones. Friends. People who love you, who love you, who love you."

"What?"

Boss, I don't know. I can't tell cuz he's so far down now, it's like shadows under water.

"Mr Hunter."

Wait…what? There were two voices, and I couldn't keep them straight. One sounded like Animal, the other was someone I didn't recognize. I couldn't tell where they were, these voices, in my head or outside.

Boss, can you hear me?

"Yeah, Animal, I…"

Boss, Kairos 'n Kronos are working on it. Doing the double-double. Speed up and regulate, but you're gonna have to stop the…

"…severe concussion. Mr. Hunter, were you involved in an accident prior to tonight's episode? Five years ago?"

Boss…you gotta

"It would appear that old wounds have reappeared, reappeared, reappeared. Phantom breaks. Psychosomatic trauma brought about by severe repression. Chronic stress disorder. You're a sick man." The last seemed to echo in my head.

I heal fast.

"How many auto accidents have you had?"

"Two." *I guess.*

"And the other one?"

"Five years ago I had one, a really bad one. Yeah, I said that."

"Tell me about it, Mr. Hunter."

I squinted at a hazy outline of a round headed man. My eyes were so heavy.

"I'm having a hard time remembering anything right now."

"Sodium amytol should help you with that."

"You got me on…?"

"You signed a waiver. Mr. Hunter, do you remember anything at all from five years ago?"

"You mean the accident on the 101?"

He shifted in his seat. I could see his outline clearly now, but it was still only a silhouette. His head kept wilting to one side and jerking back up again. A little orange light flared every now and again, illumined by a swirl of heavy smoke.

"We're trying to recover your memory: you do want that, don't you, Mr. Hunter?" He snapped his fingers.

"Yes, I want to recover my memory."

"Say you agree."

"Yes, I—"

"Consent to let me in and help." *Snap!*

"Yeah…I consent."

"Atta' boy. Atta good, good boy. Tell me about your accident five years ago then, won't you?"

I wanted to scream. I drew a blank. The old failure yawned again, like a sink-hole opening up to swallow the house.

"There's nothing there. I've already been though all this."

I heard him take a drag then swallow with a sticky, dry tongue.

"Trauma wipes memory. You are a classic schizophrenic, Mr.

Hunter. What Freud called a scissor-head. You are diseased. Lucky for you we have lab tested techniques to help millions just like you. And I will exercise them now. "

"Wait, like what?"

"Hang on one second," he said conversationally, breaking from the melodrama. Then I felt myself drifting deeper, and I knew he had just administered another dose. "I will now begin the cure."

His head lolled and, with a hand, he brought it up level again. Then he sucked in a long, deep lungful and the words burst out of him.

"Ani-maaaal!" he bellowed. "Come out! The entity called Animal, I command you out, come forth! Are you there? Signify you're there! Nowwwww!" His head quaked from the effort.

"Huh? Yeah, Boss, right here!" The words flew out of me, vomit-like.

"Animal, answer my questions!" He snapped his fingers in violent percussion.

"Yes, sir!"

"Are you inside of Thomas Hunter?" *Snap.*

"Yes." I had no control over my mouth. The operator was addressing Animal without my consent, overriding me, and gaining direct answers.

"Are you in the brain?" *Snap. Snap.*

"Yes. Yes!"

"Left or right? Left or right!?" *Clap.*

"Rrrright brain!"

I struggled to get my control back, but the drug and that wretched voice he was using—I had no power. Every question was putting him more and more in command.

"Blink the eyes!" he commanded and, unintentionally, I did.

"Lift the right hand!" I did it. He gave a series of other orders, had me lift my other arm, then each of my legs, then had me move into various sitting up and lying down positions, as though I were a push-button automaton. When he finished, he sat back and groaned with satisfaction.

"Oh, that's a good boy. I am the trainer now, aren't I, boy?"

And then my lips said it, and it was the last thing I wanted:

"Yeah, Boss, you the trainer now."

"Gooood," he said and licked his lips. "Now, Animal my boy, I want you to listen to me very carefully, you hear?"

"Yeah, Boss?" Animal said, quietly.

"STAY AWAY from THOMAS HUNTER! Acknowledge!" he screamed. "Acknowledge goddamnit!"

"Wait," I shouted, finally gaining some modicum of muscle control. "He's not the prob—"

"This self-created delusional entity is hardwired directly into the right-brain prefrontal memory matrix creating an auto-dependant psychopathic pseudo-protectorship!" he bellowed, his spittle saturating the air. "I will break it! Let the Animal go. Open the cage and let him out, goddamnit!"

"But he's not the—"

"I'm the trainer now!" *Snap. Snap. Snap.* The operator yanked control back to himself and closed me out fully. I could do nothing, a silent observer of this psychic surgery.

"You don't want to further hurt Thomas Hunter, now do you, Animal?"

It was as if my fingers were slipping from a high ledge. I felt myself growing heavier through the fog of sodium amytol and the bombastic bellows of this interloper.

"No, he's...he's my bro-brother..." I could hear the tears in Animal's quavering voice.

"And I'm *the boss!*" he proclaimed, his voice frenzied, a gospel preacher glutted on religious mania. His head thrashed in huge impossible revolutions on a neck too thin to hold it and all I could think was: *why doesn't he wear a neck brace?*

"I'm the Almighty Boss!" he shouted. "Obey! Obey! Obey!"

"Yeah...boss...you the boss!" Animal wearied inside me.

"Goooooodah." the operator brayed. "Now get the fuck out!"

"Y-You're the...the b-b—" Animal babbled under such a confusion of roles, such a loss of security.

"Animal, if you stay I will electric shock Thomas Hunter. You don't want that, do you, boy? I will shock his brain and shock you out! Shock his brain and shock you out!" He went on like that for some time. His head drooped and bobbled between breaths.

I felt Animal fade. I felt him turn from me, and then, I felt him run. I could have called him back. At that last moment, for just one fleeting instant, I could have held onto him and…I let him go.

"Hold on, Mr. Hunter, you've been, oh, so very helpful and we're almost done here, son. Just one more thing to do and you'll be home free, boy!"

Before I could protest or respond, the operator sprung to his feet, his monstrous face intersecting a high up ray of light. His eyes bulged black above a stretched jaw, as though his family line descended from deep sea fish. Dark shadows danced all about him in some trick of the light. He spread a wide hand over my chest, and screamed, "Kairos-Kronos be gowne!

"Kairos-Kronos come forward! Leave this man alone! It's good we're doing this, Mr. Hunter! Oh, so goddamn good to set you free! These auto-generated, co-dependent, delusional mind-thieves are poisoning the very waters of your soul! Let me cleanse you. Now heal, in the name of the double star! Heal, in the same of the sun god, of the moon goddess, of Horus, heeeeeeaaaaaaal!"

He heaved so that his chest inflated to some plasticized disfigurement natural bones could never allow. Currents of air rushed over me as he dragged them up, then back out again.

"Kairos-Kronos! Present! Appear! Show yourself!"

His heavy hand shook spastically on my chest, trouncing the cot and rocking my head. His other hand was planted down on his side, but I couldn't see what lay there.

I squirmed under a palm that sent cold shocks through my chest.

"Nooooaaw!" he screamed like a drunk James Brown on a Sunday morning.

"Noooooo!" I screamed, but I was too subdued to fight back.

Machine beeps ripped in a shattering staccato as my heart beat shot above human tolerance. I screamed as bone-deep stabs rippled from my skull to my femur.

"Oooooh, God!"

"Let the entity go! The pain will stop when it's gone!" he railed.

Pain flooded my nervous system. My vocal chords turned raw. My heart raced in terror. My eyes bulged. Temples swelled. Ears popped dizzyingly as the pressure built.

"Make it stop! Make it stop. Please, make it stop!"

"Cast it out!" he shrieked.

My will broke. Kairos-Kronos moved up and out, stolen from my panicked heart, in a sound like tearing fabric, leaving behind a fierce pain in my chest. And I fell. Like a suicide from a high ledge, I fell into darkness, into nowhere.

"...keep him drugged and cover up that eye...with the patch... the patch..." The words were spoken to others I hadn't known were in the room. "And don't hurt him."

And then *silence*...

...and nothing

Chapter 18

I was floating in blackness and before me loomed a brilliant blue light. I moved towards it, closer and closer, until it filled my whole vision.

Come home, it told me. *Hunter, come home.*

ㄱㅐㅓ·ㅣㄱ

I woke in a hospital bed. A serving of chicken a la king and green jello sat on my bed stand. IV tubes hung from clear, plastic bags and a bird was chirping outside.

"Good morning," said a voice, which belonged to a young nurse who seemed overly fond of cherry red lipstick. To be fair, she was pleasant enough to look at and didn't do anything other than check my forehead and wink. "Feeling better?" she asked.

"Um, yeah," I replied. "I'm fine."

"Oh, good. We should have you on your way in a couple of hours max."

"Oh, yeah?"

"Yup. After the psych eval." She was already walking out. "By the way, you say a lot of interesting things when you take morphine." Then she disappeared. I wasn't sure if I should read that as a harmless flirt, or something more sinister. Either way, she got me wondering what the hell I'd said. The psych evaluation lasted about twenty minutes.

"You'll begin to feel more yourself as time passes," Dr. Patel said. "You may feel lonely for a while at first, you've had a lot of voices in your head."

I nodded at that. "That's putting it mildly."

Patel shrugged. "We all have demons, Mr. Hunter. Just some of us have stronger ones. And yours were extremely strong. You see these?" He pushed forward a file and opened it. X-rays.

"Yes," I said.

"Well, these are not my specialty, but I called for them since your case is highly irregular. Look here, in these you can see the fractures all throughout your neck and spine here. But in these, taken after the entities were rooted out, you see, there is nothing. No hairline breaks. You see?"

I looked closer. I did see the difference. "What does it mean?"

"It means, Mr. Hunter, you've had—forgive me this expression—phantom bone fractures."

I shook my head. "I don't get it."

"Psychosomatic bone breaks. It's astounding. I have never seen a case like this. We have often seen hypochondriacs complain of these kinds of things, but you know, that is just imagination gone crazy. But you, you had it. Proof is right here. You have it, then you don't have it. Entities in this one, no entities in that one. You see?"

I sat back and laughed in disbelief. "They were doing that to me?" I pointed at the x-rays.

He nodded his head. "They were, um, parasitic. They kept you broken, but then also regulated your system so that you didn't feel the pain. Does that make sense? They kept you sick, basically, but didn't let your brain tell you about it."

"That's unreal."

"Very," he agreed. "But now, you're healthy. You're a medical miracle, you know that?"

"Thank you, doctor, thank you very much."

"You're quite welcome, Mr. Hunter. If you have any questions, come back to see me. Okay? Thank you."

Half an hour later, when Avril walked into the lobby, she stepped right into my arms and hugged me.

"I love you," she said.

"How are you feeling?" I asked. "You okay?"

"I'm actually really good. I guess I just needed sleep," she said, chuckling. "How are you?"

"I'm…fine. No, it's strange and odd and…but, I'm okay. I mean, I feel good."

She smiled. "Good."

Avril had passed out from exhaustion. That had been the cause of the accident. She would be fine with a few weeks rest. And me too. That's what the doctors had ordered. Let the police take the burden for a while. In a few weeks, a month maybe, help them if you want.

I could agree to that, for now anyway. I didn't know if I would have felt differently if I'd still had my crew. Who can say? Regardless, I had a lot to get used to. No Animal whispering his base intentions in my ear, for one. My eye had a patch over it, too. It would heal, the doctors said, but I knew what a patch meant: no Third.

The ramifications of all this made me...happy? Only time would tell.

ㅋ ﬆ ꓘ⍺

"I have a daughter," Avril said casually as we drove into town.

"What? Who with?"

She laughed. "A low life. It was before I ever got involved with Eddy."

"Wow, you never said anything."

"Yeah, I just thought of it. I mean, it didn't seem relevant before. We had a lot of other things going on."

"How old?"

"She is, oh God, you know how it is with kids. They grow up so fast. Twelve, I guess."

"I bet she's beautiful. Is she at the house?"

"She lives with me if that's what you're asking. Staying with her grandmother at the moment, but you'll meet her tomorrow."

We had driven to Avril's summer home outside of Pacifica, California in the small town of San Ragita. I'd never heard of San Ragita, but that's not saying anything. "Quaint" didn't even begin. Rows of coffee shops, pancake houses, tobacconists, byzantine jewelry markets and old-time peanut stands stacked the streets like Victorian era London.

We walked through the crooked streets, past a myriad of performers: musicians, painters, sleight of hand magicians, chess players, jugglers and one fire eater.

"Seriously, a fire eater?"

Pastry shops served up apple fritters, crumpets, deep fried waffles, crepes and anything else you could ever want. Coffee roasters brewed banana coffee and Mexican chocolate espresso with heaps of whipped cream, cinnamon and nutmeg. All manner of beautiful and vibrant human beings swarmed these streets, most of whom were physically fit.

"They have an ordinance in this town…" Avril was saying as a group of young women wearing bohemian skirts, sandals and nothing else sauntered past us. I was helpless to avert my gaze.

"…that women can go topless once a week."

Giggling and eating ice cream, shaking her tresses, one nubile beauty eyed me as she passed. She couldn't have been a day over eighteen and those red, ringlet curls and those lips, pushing down on that cone—Jesus Henry Christ!

"Come on," Avril pulled me through the crowd, around an exceptionally fit man on four-foot stilts, into The Corner Bookery.

"I love this place," she announced.

I have to admit I was relieved to be surrounded by heaps of sexless books. Inside, rows and piles slopped haphazardly through its many nooks. A young man with a kinky beard and a monocle looked up from behind the counter. He smiled and went back to his reading. We emerged through some near-tunnels into an open serving area, where coffee and pastries were being dished up by three young women, fully clothed, but braless and beautiful. All blondes.

Avril ordered two Spanish mochas because "they use Gibralter chocolate and real Valencia orange oil and you just don't get this anywhere else in the world" and a plate full of scones. The mochas came in big, bowl-like cups with whipped cream slopping over the sides and chocolate cookie straws sticking out the tops. Mine had a gingerbread man floating in there, too.

"My God, Avril, this place is freaking unreal!"

We wound around some edifice of old tomes—the kind that make you want to hole up in a musty library for a good month or two and just read everything you can get your hands on—and found a booth. Of course, it was private in the extreme, with lamps and candles and soft cushions. The scent of flavored cigar smoke soaked deep into the wood.

"Can you smoke in here?"

"I think so," she said. "Oh, yeah, duh." She pushed the ashtray toward me.

We drank our mochas, which were beyond amazing, and smoked Turkish cigarettes and generally felt extremely satisfied. At one point, a waitress came and asked if we needed anything and then gave us her number and told us to text her if we did because otherwise she planned to leave us alone.

"So, how long are we going to stay? In San Ragita, I mean."

Avril shrugged. "As long as you want."

I smiled. The lamplight was catching her eyes in a way that gave beauty a new definition.

"I don't know," I said. "Place is really incredible. I feel like I could live the rest of my life here." The true sentiment was a near polar opposite, I felt like I could die here, fulfilled at last.

"I'm glad you like it."

At that moment, something came over me so strong that I knew it was the right thing. I didn't even have to think it over.

"Avril," I said.

"Yeah?"

"Will you marry me?"

She giggled. "Are you serious?"

"Actually, yeah, I am." I laughed, hardly believing it myself.

She mulled it over, and then said, "Only if you promise me something."

"Anything."

She took a deep breath and her smile seemed to fade ever so slightly.

"That you never try to get your crew back."

Read
CHAPEL PERILOUS,
THOMAS HUNTER FILES, VOL. II

By

Andrew Michael Schwarz

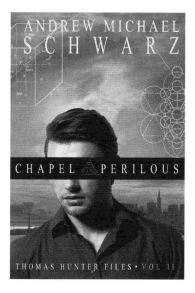

The case just got personal.

Avril and I walked away from the accident without a scratch. Now, we're getting married in a quaint and cozy village on the edge of the sea. It seems I can finally get my life back.

But...

I find myself living an existence that can't possibly be mine. I find myself in love, domestic...restless. I have all that I could ever want, except the one thing I need: my crew.

It means I'm defenseless.

The doctors assure me this is for the best. They tell me my crew was a disease. I don't believe them. Little things add up and my discontent grows. My suspicion leads me to investigate.
Things aren't what they seem.

My fate is linked to Incorruptibles, to black magick conspiracies, to those who would keep me subdued.

And so I walk alone into Chapel Perilous, that state in which the occult and the mundane ride side by side, where death is imminent and the loss of sanity a constant threat.

This case is personal, its debt is severe.
Its resolution is my only option.

ABOUT THE AUTHOR

Andrew Michael Schwarz is an active member of the Oregon Coast Writer's Network and an initiate of the Red Sneaker Writer's school. He is a writer, publisher, public speaker and graphic designer. He is also a trained investigator and has personally logged hundreds of hours of covert surveillance for private industry and government offices.

LEARN ABOUT NEW RELEASES

http://andrewmichaelschwarz.com/newsletter/

FIND ME ONLINE

https://www.facebook.com/andy.schwarz.96
https://twitter.com/amichaelschwarz
https://www.goodreads.com/AMichaelSchwarz
amichaelschwarz@gmail.com

Printed in Great Britain
by Amazon

85396706R00112